Jo Macauley

Secrets
&
Spies

Plague

With special thanks to Adrian Bott

First published in 2013 by Curious Fox,
an imprint of Capstone Global Library Limited,
7 Pilgrim Street, London, EC4V 6LB
Registered company number: 6695582

www.curious-fox.com

Text © Hothouse Fiction Ltd 2013

Series created by Hothouse Fiction
www.hothousefiction.com

The author's moral rights are hereby asserted.

Cover design by samcombes.co.uk

ISBN 978 1 78202 041 7

1 3 5 7 9 10 8 6 4 2

A CIP catalogue for this book is available from the British Library.

Typeset in Adobe Garamond Pro by Hothouse Fiction Ltd

Printed and bound by CPI Group (UK) Ltd, Croydon, CR0 4YY

For Sabrina

Prologue
London, August 1665

Death walked the streets of London, visiting households unseen in the night, and leaving bodies stiff in their sheets by morning.

The tell-tale red marks of the plague appeared without warning on living flesh, branding it as Death's own. As if the disease had been a demon or a vampire, people attempted to ward it off with herbs, prayers and mystic signs. Even learned men walked with folded abracadabra-papers in their pockets, but none of these measures seemed to slow the plague's progress.

Inside the Four Swans tavern, which lay deep in the

nested streets of the city, the atmosphere was stifling and airless. The windows were shut fast even in the baking heat of August, for fear that the stench of plague would enter and carry the disease with it. Tempers flared like hot coals, and an argument was growing loud in the half-empty bar. Already the other drinkers had begun to shift their chairs away.

Tam Dixon swigged at his ale and glared with bloodshot eyes at his two companions.

"I'll not be mocked! You're always mocking me! The pair of you, in fact. One more word and I'll crack your heads together, don't think I won't!"

"You couldn't crack the head of a louse, you great lump," sneered Martin, one of his erstwhile friends. "Sit down and drink."

Tam hesitated, swaying from the alcohol, fuming like a powder keg ready to explode. He didn't pay any attention to the thin, hollow-cheeked man who sat only an arm's length away behind him. The man had been there all evening, apparently waiting for a companion to join him – at least, that was the message implied by the hat he'd left on a neighbouring chair, as though he were saving it for someone.

Just as Tam seemed about to sit back down, a fly

settled on the lip of his beer mug.

Jack Hardy couldn't resist. "Now there's a drinker who can hold his beer better than Tam!" He roared with laughter.

The table went flying over. Mugs shattered and a serving girl gave a theatrical scream. Martin and Jack were on their feet in seconds. Tam swung for Jack first. Fist met face with a resounding smack, and as Jack went staggering back through the chairs, Martin leaped and grabbed Tam round the neck. Tam roared and swung Martin back and forth, trying to loosen the stranglehold. Martin, teeth bared, hung on grimly. In the background, Jack coughed and spat a bloodied tooth onto the floor. The thin man, meanwhile, simply sat and watched the fight happen right in front of him, as if he were too much of a fool to move out of the way. He was very good at appearing foolish.

He had put a lot of work into it while training as a spy.

Tam thumped Martin hard in the guts, finally breaking his grip. As Martin fell backward, the thin man leaped to his feet and caught him before he could hit the floor.

"Steady, there!" he said, patting Martin on the

shoulder. His other hand slipped into Martin's pocket as fast as a striking adder. The afflicted man didn't notice. Nobody did. The movement was as quick as the flicker of an eyelash, and drew about as much attention. The spy's thin fingers closed on a small piece of paper. *The prize. At last.*

Martin shoved himself away without so much as a thank you, and the spy gave an offended harrumph. Clapping his hat upon his head, he left the tavern without looking back. The paper was still in his clenched hand, curled tight as a clock spring.

One little twist of paper could do a lot of things, the spy thought to himself as he hurried through the London streets. It could entitle you to a fortune, or strip you of one. The right words, with the right signature beneath, could condemn a man to death. And once in a while, a single scrap of paper like this could be the fuse that lit the gunpowder and blew a whole city sky-high.

Moments later, the spy brushed past his master at the agreed place. The paper changed hands safely. Once his master had gone, the thin man drew out a handkerchief with shaking hands and wiped nervous sweat from his forehead. For such a tiny thing, the paper had been a monstrous weight to carry.

His heart lighter now, he made his way back through the streets, heading for home. A quick glance over his shoulder told him he wasn't being followed. If it hadn't been for the groans of the dying and the pale bodies lying unburied by the roadside, he might have whistled a merry tune.

He turned down a side street. Home was only a stone's throw away now, and he thought with relish of the cold ham and the keg of beer waiting for him…

From behind came the sound of footsteps, hurrying up swiftly.

The spy frowned. Suddenly, he was no longer sure he hadn't been followed. He was no longer sure of anything. He began to turn round, but he never saw his attacker. The last thing he felt was an agonizing blow to the head.

Then there was only the sound of a body being dragged away over the cobblestones…

Chapter One

A Surprise Announcement

"Is it *very* bad, Miss Beth?"

Beth Johnson, dressed in a pastel-blue shepherdess costume, her chestnut-coloured curls done up in bows, sighed as she peeked through the curtains into the theatre. "Well … I've seen emptier houses on a first night. But not often."

Maisie White, the theatre's orange-seller and Beth's young friend, peered up at her with wide, concerned eyes, her face framed by her own brown ringlets.

"That means bad, don't it?"

"Shh! You must whisper backstage. Do you not

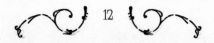

have fruit to sell?" Beth's fellow actor, Benjamin Lovett, muttered at Maisie as he strode by adjusting his costume.

"There's hardly anyone to buy them," Maisie retorted, shifting the basket of oranges on her hip.

Beth turned to Maisie and gave her an encouraging smile. "It's not looking very full out there, that is true. But they're still our audience, large or small, and the show must go on."

Maisie looked doubtful. "But Mister Huntingdon was saying we need the numbers if we're ever going to stay open…"

"Hush, now," Beth scolded her lightly. "We mustn't complain of empty seats in our dear theatre. Not when there are empty seats around so many families' dinner tables."

But as Beth peeped once more through the gap in the curtains at the rows of empty seats, dotted here and there with troubled-looking faces, the sight wrenched at her heart. This would be a tough crowd to entertain, and she couldn't blame them one bit. It was just as well, she thought, that tonight's show was a romantic comedy. It was the first night of *Love's Green Garlands, or Trust Repaid*, a light-hearted piece on the good old reliable themes of mistaken identity, messages misunderstood, long-lost sweethearts reunited and true love triumphant in the end.

William Huntingdon, the well-respected theatre manager, ambled up. "Three minutes to curtain, you lot. Look lively!"

"I hope to goodness that there isn't any plague where my father is," Maisie said. "It's not *everywhere*, is it, Miss Beth?"

"Not at all," Beth said, reaching an arm around her young friend and squeezing her shoulders. "We just have to keep faith that he, and everyone we love, will be all right."

Maisie nodded and smiled bravely, but there was little hope left in her eyes. Born in the Americas, the daughter of a convict mother now dead, ten-year-old Maisie longed to find her father in London.

Beth took a deep breath. She expected a few of the audience to at least look excited in the last moments before the curtain went up, but there still wasn't a smile to be seen on any of the faces out there.

"Just pretend you're playing to a packed house," her aged actor friend Brian Appleworth told her. "You'll have them wetting themselves, plague or no plague."

"Please stop saying that word, Mister Appleworth,"

shivered Maisie. "You can call it in upon yourself if you name it."

"Don't be preposterous, girl," said Lovett scornfully, squeezing past them to get his own look at the audience before the curtain went up. As Beth's devoted rival, he could be counted upon to put in an unkind word for her – or her friends. "The plague's a disease like any other, borne upon the air. It's not some night-hag out of your story books that has to be called over the threshold!"

"I reckon it's the Dutch who are behind it," Brian said thoughtfully. "We're at war with them now, aren't we? So it stands to reason. Who but the Dutch stand to gain by wiping out the English?"

"Everybody, hush!" barked Mr Huntingdon. "Curtain up!"

Beth bounded onto the stage, her brown curls flying. Scattered applause greeted her as the audience recognized her as the young actress most of them had come to see.

"Oh, little lambs!" she cried, shading her eyes as she looked around. "Oh, whither have you strayed? Be not affrighted, sweet and tender lambs! I'll seek you out and lead you safely home, from out the grasp of this unwholesome wood!"

A few hesitant laughs came from the audience. They

could tell she was playing a lovely young shepherdess whose lambs had gone wandering, but she meant her words to comfort *them* too.

That's the way, Beth thought. *I'll cheer you up if it takes me all night.*

With open arms and a sweet smile she set to work, delivering her lines in such merry, soothing tones that the audience soon began to smile back at her. It was working – but she had to wonder how long she could make the happy mood last. At the end of her next speech the prince would cross the shepherdess's path, and by the looks of Lovett, he couldn't wait to upstage her.

Well, let him wait!

Instead of finishing her speech, Beth led the audience into a song, one she was sure they would know. She couldn't sing to save her life, but she cued them in with the words: "Down in a glade, diddle diddle, where flowers do grow…"

Sure enough, some of the voices began to sing. "And the trees bud, diddle diddle," they sang back to her, "all in a row…"

Beth conducted them with her hands, smiling brightly, while Lovett glared from the wings like a fierce bull penned up in a field. "She can't do that!" Beth heard him hiss furiously to Huntingdon. "Those aren't her lines!"

"Shepherdesses *have* been known to demand a song or two, Benjamin," the theatre manager said, with just the hint of a smile. "In fact, they're rather renowned for it."

"But she's mutilating the script!"

"Ah, yes, the script," said Huntingdon dryly. "I shall make sure that the song is written in for all future performances. It suits the scene rather well."

Lovett had clearly heard enough. Swirling his cape around him, he strode out onto the stage, right in front of Beth who was about to lead the audience into another chorus.

"WHO SKIPS SO PRETTILY THROUGH THIS DANK WOOD?" he boomed.

Beth bit her lip with rage. Lovett had moaned about *her* changing the script, but those weren't even his proper opening lines! The prince was supposed to say "Wait, gentle maid, I'll do to thee no harm," but Lovett clearly had other ideas. He held his cape up over his arm so that it hung in front of Beth like a second stage curtain.

"Some nymph it is, with more than mortal grace! But wherefore dost thou hide, my bonny one?"

Beth wanted to scream "I'm behind you, you stage-hogging trout!" But if she lost her temper, Lovett would have won. Instead, she skipped out from behind his cape.

"For fear that I should come to dreadful harm," she ad-libbed. "For robbers lurk and brigands wait to pounce … but hold! Art thou not prince of all these lands?"

Now it was Lovett's turn to flounder as he tried to come up with a line.

Beth couldn't resist. "I fear this man has forgot who he is," she told the audience with a shrug. That got a hearty laugh.

Lovett looked desperately to the prompter, who gave him a helpless look. *Serves him right for making up his own lines*, Beth thought.

"Indeed I am the prince of, er … all these lands," Lovett said. He crossed the stage to stand in front of Beth once again, and began to recite his long speech about what a fancy castle he lived in, but how his real passion was to wander in the woods disguised as a common peasant. Lovett started to add more made-up lines, with pompous details about his royal forefathers and the heavy burden of being heir to the throne.

Beth wasn't having that. She yawned loudly, bringing the speech to a sudden halt. That brought more chuckles

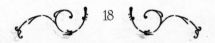

from the audience and a red face from Lovett.

From that point on, it was war. Lovett did everything he could to wrong-foot her – hogging the stage, feeding her the wrong lines, even standing on her toe. Beth bounced back from everything he threw at her, keeping the audience entertained with witty asides until they were eating out of her hand.

As the scene drew to a close, Beth felt triumphant. *We've done it*, she thought. *We can't cure the plague, but we've proved we can help people forget their troubles, even if it's only for a couple of hours.*

Lovett had given up trying to throw her off, thank goodness. "Sleep now, sweet maid, upon this mossy bank," he said, "'til love shall wake thee when I do return. Let prince's royal garb make soft thy rest."

Beth lay down against the painted scenery and Lovett unfastened his velvet cloak, kneeling down to drape it over her. The audience held their breath. She felt the heavy warmth of the cloak settle on her body and crossed her fingers, hoping for a storm of applause as the curtain fell.

"PLAGUE!"

The shriek had come from the front row of the audience. Lovett stood stupefied, staring out over the

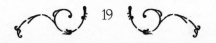

half-filled theatre, completely at a loss.

"Look at his arms!" the woman screamed. "It's the rash! The red roses!"

Beth pulled the cloak away from her face and saw what the woman was pointing at. All the way up Lovett's bared arms were red blotches, as if cruel fingers had pinched the skin hard.

"Plague!" the scream went up, spreading throughout the audience. "Plague!" People were stampeding into the aisles now, running for the exit.

"Wait!" Lovett demanded. "It's not the plague, you fools! It's nothing but louse bites! These rotten cheap costumes they make me wear, they're full of lice!"

Beth sprang to her feet. Without a thought for her own safety, she grabbed Lovett's arm and looked closely. The scarlet marks on his skin were ugly, but they were nothing like the sores that had appeared on the plague victims. Lovett was telling the truth.

"Everyone, please!" she begged. "There's no plague here! Calm down!"

The audience ignored them completely. The terror of the plague had seized their hearts and minds, and Beth and Lovett could do nothing but look on, united for once in their helpless misery, as the theatre emptied

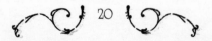

around them. Less than a minute had passed before the last panicked theatregoer crashed their way through the doors and out into the streets. Beth sat down heavily, her skirts rumpling around her. Lovett joined her, swinging his heels over the edge of the stage like a heartbroken schoolboy on a swing.

The rest of the cast slowly filtered onto the stage, looking out at the empty auditorium as if they had to see for themselves how bad it was. Young Robert looked like he was about to cry. Maisie was shaking her head, quietly saying "I told him it was bad luck."

"Philistines," Lovett said bitterly. "My talents are wasted on the likes of them. What's London, anyway? A provincial village on a muddy old river, that's what."

"They're afraid!" Beth said angrily. "Everyone in this city is. You might not take the plague seriously, but they do!"

"Seriously enough to run like rats from a sinking ship," Lovett said scornfully. "Just for the sight of a few louse bites. Idiots."

"Tired of London, are we, Benjamin?" said Huntingdon, with a dark look on his face. He was tapping a letter into the palm of his hand. "Well, you'll be glad to hear you won't be here for much longer."

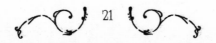

21

Beth gaped. Lovett had finally done it. He'd upstaged her once too often, and Huntingdon was dismissing him from the company!

"What?" Lovett blustered. "L-leave London?"

"Our patron, His Majesty the King, has sent us a command under the royal seal," declared Huntingdon, holding up the letter for all to see. "While the plague is rampant in London, it is no longer safe for us to stay here. We are to leave for Oxford on the morrow."

"Tomorrow morning?" Beth burst out. "But we can't leave - we've advertised other performances! People will come here, expecting us. The play's only just opened!"

"I'm sorry, Beth," said Huntingdon. "It was a good play. It deserved a better run. You all did your best."

Murmuring to one another quietly, the subdued company made their way out of the theatre. Beth and Maisie left by the stage door, with Beth feeling like she had to slip out quietly, in case she was seen after the disaster of the abandoned play.

"What if Big Moll catches the plague?" Maisie kept saying. "Or ... or I don't know, perhaps the Peacock and Pie could burn down while we're away? We could find ourselves with no home, no landlady…"

"We can't worry about such things," Beth said. "We've

 22

got enough on our hands. I have to pack, box up my things, I've letters to send…"

"Won't be time to send any letters, Miss Beth," said Maisie gloomily. "Besides, where would you find a messenger to take it for you?"

Maisie was right, Beth realized. Her vision of writing a hasty letter to John Turner by candlelight evaporated.

John, who had formed such a bond of trust with her on her last mission. John, her friend and now her fellow spy, along with the vagabond Ralph Chandler. Nobody in the theatre company knew of her secret mission to serve and protect the King under the guidance of their spymaster, Sir Alan Strange. Ralph had been taken in by Strange and trained in the art of espionage long before Beth had met either of them, but John had only stumbled into their world by chance. And yet he'd been an integral part of their mission to stop the recent attempt on the King's life, and as such had been invited to join their gang of spies.

But it could be some time before even their spymaster knew of the company's move to Oxford.

Unless word got back to them soon, John would be looking for her, wondering where she was, in a city full of deadly disease, and she had no way to let him

know where she'd gone. In spite of her hopes to keep her thoughts professional, Beth's heart sank at the idea that he might think she'd abandoned him without word.

Later, as Beth made her way back through the streets to her home at the Peacock and Pie tavern, the threat of the plague seemed to loom ever larger. She couldn't help noticing more glaringly the desperate sobs of women who'd no doubt just been told terrible news about their loved ones, or the furtive glances of people at the merest hint of their companion coughing or sneezing. Instead, she looked up at the familiar rooftops and high windows of London, trying to fix them in her mind. The future had become suddenly uncertain, and those memories might be all she ever had to come home to if this terrible disease continued.

Who knew if she might ever return to London again?

Chapter Two
A New Addition

At first, Beth had thought the two-day journey to Oxford might be a pleasant one. Open country, sunny skies – it couldn't be too bad, could it? But the first sight of the transport Huntingdon had arranged quickly put an end to that notion.

"Ah – open carts," she said, trying not to sound too dismayed as she looked at the high-sided wooden carts with their long benches on either side. "They look … er … what's the word?"

"Filthy," Maisie muttered.

"Rustic!" Beth corrected her quickly. "So we're

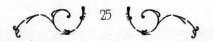

travelling country-style. I should have kept my shepherdess costume on! Besides, Maisie, I know you're glad just to be coming along with the company at all," she said to her friend pointedly. Maisie nodded quickly and began to clamber onto one of the carts without another word.

"They were the best I could get at short notice and with next to no money," Huntingdon told Beth apologetically. "Comfort will have to wait until we're in Oxford. 'Til then, I'd find a bale of hay to sit on if I were you."

The hours of travel passed all too slowly. The English countryside was green and blooming all right, but the road was so cracked and dry from the heat that dust rose up in choking clouds from the carts in front. Beth felt grimed and gritty all over, not to mention sore from the constant jolts and judders.

The company stopped at a coaching inn in High Wycombe to spend the night, and Beth gratefully went to splash some cool water on her face. As she was making her way back to her table, she overheard Lovett complaining to Huntingdon at the foot of the stairs:

"...any idea of the problems we've had since we brought *one* woman into the company? Diplomacy is all very well, but surely under the circumstances…"

Going unnoticed to eavesdrop was part of her spy training, but Beth knew that if she stayed to listen to any more, they'd find her out. Reluctantly, she continued her journey back to her table, frowning with irritation. Dozens of questions were boiling up within her as she ate her simple dinner of bread, goat's cheese and dark bitter ale. Lovett bellyaching about her was nothing new, but he'd never made *this* complaint before. She couldn't stop thinking about the way he'd said the words, "since we brought *one* woman into the company." Obviously, Lovett objected to any woman acting alongside him, so the implication was that there might soon be *more* than one.

Could Huntingdon really be thinking of bringing more female actors on board? He wasn't considering cutting Beth's roles down, surely … So far as she knew, he'd been delighted with her performances. And what on earth did "diplomacy" have to do with it? She thought about the fact that her position at the theatre was useful cover for her work as a spy. Could there be another of Alan Strange's recruits being drafted in without her knowledge? Beth sighed – she hated not knowing what was going on.

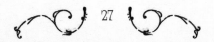

* * *

Another exhausting day on the road followed the first, and it was growing late when the King's Company finally rolled into Oxford. Beth had heard it was a beautiful city, but the sight of the spires and the gleaming river coming into view was so lovely it went quite some way to make up for the arduous journey there.

"No wonder the King's chosen to move his court here!" she laughed, as a light evening breeze ruffled her hair. "In all this red and golden light, it looks like something out of a fairytale book."

"Oxford's long been a friend to His Majesty," said Brian. "This is where his father Charles I lived during the war against Cromwell's lot."

"Of course!" said Beth. "Oxford was Royalist through and through, wasn't it?"

"Mostly," Brian said casually. "His Majesty spent many years here. It's like a second home to him."

As the carts drew wearily into the Oxford streets, Beth was glad to see they were clean and quiet. She was braced for her first sight of a red cross on a door, but there was no sign of any. The plague really seemed to have passed

Oxford by – at least for now. The carts clattered to a halt in the broad courtyard of an inn. It was a huge building, close to the river, with many sloping roofs and cosy-looking casement windows.

"The Half Moon Inn," she read, looking up at the painted sign and nudging Maisie, who'd actually managed to fall asleep on the juddering cart. "Home sweet home, for now at least."

Even Lovett seemed satisfied. "This is more like it! It's good to be back in dear old Oxford at last. When I think of the nights I spent here as a student! All the scrapes, the tomfoolery, the dares…" He looked around wistfully. "The things we got up to would make the ladies swoon!"

"Well, try to restrain yourself while we're staying here," Huntingdon said wryly. "We're the King's Company, don't forget, and we've an important duty to carry out."

Beth had to speak up. "Duty? I thought we were just here to lodge for a while, until London was safe to return to?"

Huntingdon gave her a tired smile as if he'd said too much. "We still have to earn our keep, Beth," he said. "Tomorrow we'll find out more, but for now … let's just say there's a strong chance *Love's Green Garlands* will see more than one performance after all."

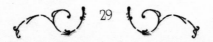

29

The next morning, the whole company gathered at Christ Church, the magnificent college where King Charles I had stayed. They sat down to breakfast in the Great Hall, and Beth watched Maisie's wide-eyed amazement with relish. She too marvelled at its long tables, huge portraits and high vaulted ceiling. The building had a wonderful antique smell, a sort of dusky blend of polished wood, old books, leather and frankincense, as if it were half-library, half-cathedral. She could hardly contain her excitement. Something was clearly afoot, and she was finally on the verge of discovering what it was.

"Lord Wilmot, Second Earl of Rochester!" announced the steward who was haunting the doorway. The company quickly got to their feet.

Beth stared as a young man of about eighteen came striding into the room, wearing a colossal wig, a frock coat and an expression of deep mischief. His eyes locked with hers instantly, and she felt an uneasy lurch behind her ribs.

"Actors!" he said with relish, like a starving man might

say "food."

The whole company bowed and curtsied, Beth along with them, but Lord Wilmot never took his eyes off her. She began to feel heat stealing across her face, but Huntingdon came to her rescue.

"Your Grace, may I introduce the King's Company of Drury Lane. We are His Majesty's humble servants."

"Aren't we all," said Lord Wilmot. "Sit, sit. Regrettably His Majesty cannot join us in person, but he bids you welcome to Oxford. He hopes this move from London will not have to be permanent." He steepled his fingers. "Can't say I agree. I'd *love* to keep you here."

"You enjoy the theatre, Your Grace?" Beth said boldly.

Lord Wilmot grinned like a hungry fox. "Immensely."

"Word of Your Grace's appetite has reached Drury Lane," said Huntingdon, giving Beth a warning glance.

Lord Wilmot waved a dismissive hand. "I dabble. Now, to the point. While you remain here, Master Huntingdon, your company has an emergency role. You will entertain His Majesty's court while we remain resident in Oxford."

Huntingdon smiled and nodded. "I am sure I speak for us all when I say it will be our pleasure."

Wilmot nodded. "His Majesty expressly requires you

to perform *Love's Green Garlands* exactly as you would have done at home … with one small alteration."

He let that ominous statement hang in the air for a moment. *He's enjoying this*, Beth realized. He may have been an earl by birth, but Lord Wilmot was clearly a performer through and through.

"His Majesty's cousin, Lady Lucy Joseph, is lately come to England from Germany," Wilmot went on. "But as it is still too dangerous for her in London, she will be coming here to Oxford. *And* as she has a keen interest in the theatre, it would please His Majesty greatly if she could be given a part in your play. A small part would suffice."

"Indeed. I am sure we can accommodate," Huntingdon said through a strained smile.

He didn't look at all surprised, and Beth realized he must have been expecting this. She glanced quickly at Lovett, and there was barely-hidden anger written all over his face. So *that* was what he had been complaining about the previous night. Another actress in the company – and the King's cousin, no less.

"It is very important that young Lady Lucy be kept happy," Wilmot said smoothly, though with a hint of menace.

 32

"Naturally," Huntingdon said.

Wilmot studied him, and then nodded curtly. They understood one another.

The facts slotted into place in Beth's mind like puzzle pieces. *Diplomacy.* Beth had heard of Lady Lucy, cousin to the King, who had spent her childhood at the court of the German monarch. With England at war with Holland, she realized that the King must be trying to form alliances with other countries of Europe – and Germany would certainly make a strong ally. Beth decided that Lucy must be well-loved in the German court, if the King hoped to build an alliance on the basis of her ambassadorship. Her good will – or her anger – could have consequences for the potential alliance, and for all England itself.

"I'll leave you to it, then," Lord Wilmot said. "Good day to you all. I am eager, nay, *ravenous* to see you perform for us here at Christ Church." He took a step closer to Beth, and she cringed inwardly. "Especially the *delectable* Miss Johnson. I'm sure I shall savour her appearance for a very long time…"

* * *

Beth was unpacking her things, helped by Maisie, with whom she was sharing a room, when there was a knock on the door.

"I wanted to have a quiet word," Huntingdon said when she admitted him. He glanced at Maisie, who she saw was pretending not to be listening while smoothing out some of Beth's dresses.

"About Lady Lucy?" Beth guessed.

"She's twelve, Beth. A fair bit younger than you, but you're the best person I can think of to look after her." He held up his hands. "Court diplomacy is a difficult matter. It requires the right person. I've never been a twelve-year-old girl. You have. And believe me, I wouldn't ask you unless it was important. There are reasons—"

"I'd be happy to take care of her," Beth assured him quickly. "Leave it to me."

"She's an enthusiastic amateur actress," Huntingdon said, enunciating every word. He pulled off his wig and fanned himself. To her alarm, Beth saw he was sweating. "She might be a natural, God willing, but then again, she might be a disaster…"

"So long as she *enjoys* acting with us," Beth ventured, "does it really matter if she's any good at it? After all, isn't the important thing to keep her happy?"

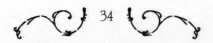

Huntingdon paused and gave her a long appraising look. "You're a very good listener, Beth Johnson. The kind who sometimes hears what people don't say out loud."

Beth grinned. "I'll make sure she has all the fun a girl her age could want."

When Huntingdon left, she turned back into the room and saw Maisie sitting on the end of the bed, pouting and swinging her legs. She remembered her young friend had aspirations to follow in her footsteps and become an actress too.

"There's no need for that sour face, young Maisie," Beth said. "You'll get your chance at the stage one day too! For now, we have to do everything we can to make sure the King's cousin is welcomed into the company…"

Lady Lucy Joseph had a face like a china doll. Her painted-on eyebrows were arched ridiculously high, her chin was narrow, and her skin had the palest white look of the finest porcelain.

Beth watched her as the young girl sat backstage, smearing even more foundation onto her face on top of

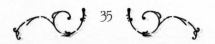

the ludicrous amount that already clung there. The hand-held mirror she was looking into was exquisite, its carved wooden surround a masterpiece of fine carpentry. Beth cleared her throat, announcing her presence politely, and Lucy turned round slowly, like some strange girl-sized marionette.

"Hello. I'm Beth Johnson. Lovely to meet you," she said, smiling.

Lucy inclined her head, looking even more like a puppet; Beth half expected to see strings holding her arms and legs up. She forced herself to smile more widely and stepped forwards. "I'm looking forward to helping you get to know the play. And if there's any help I can give with the acting side, I'd be glad to. You may even have the opportunity to perform for your cousin, the King, himself!"

"That matters little to me," Lady Lucy said in a cold, flat voice that held a clear German accent, despite her perfect English. "I act for the craft. Though perhaps being in the King's Company could have its uses…"

Beth frowned a little at this. "Oh. Well, that is fair; I suppose you mustn't worry about who is watching, really. The important thing about acting is to enjoy yourself." Beth reached over to touch Lucy's mirror, with its gorgeous frame. "Isn't this beautiful? You must be very—"

Lucy jerked it away from her fingers. "You shall *not* touch it!" she snapped.

Taken aback, Beth could only blurt, "I'm sorry!"

"This was carved by a German master artisan," Lucy sneered. "It is the only one of its kind, and I was the only one deemed worthy of owning it. It's far more valuable than anything you will ever own. And as for you teaching me anything about this play?" She threw back her head and gave a high-pitched laugh like a whinnying filly as Beth stared at her. "You must understand that I have an outstanding reputation abroad for my acting. You can teach me nothing. Instead, it is *you* who will learn from *me*, Miss Johnson!"

Chapter Three

A Welcome Summons

Midway through the next day, and Beth's acting ability was facing its toughest challenge ever. Never had she had to work so hard just to put on a sunny disposition. *This is important*, she told herself. *Think of the treaty with Germany … Think of what Alan Strange would expect of his spies … Think of the King!*

Far from being the shy amateur Beth had expected her to be, Lady Lucy was proving to be a living nightmare. She was rude, bossy, arrogant and – in Beth's opinion – badly in need of a twisted ear to bring her in line. Beth had to draw on every last ounce of her skill to avoid losing her temper with the girl.

The first rehearsal was proving a disaster. In fact, the rehearsal had barely begun before the troubles started. Lucy had been cast as a princess in the royal court, which seemed a nice touch, Beth thought, flattering the girl's pretensions. In the scene she was meant to be rehearsing, Beth's shepherdess had crept to the palace to visit her prince in secret, only to wake up the startled princess instead. Lucy had been escorted to her place, a seat behind a scenery window. The idea was that the princess would look down from her turret, see the shepherdess creeping about, and challenge her. The prince would then appear, order the princess back to bed, and the secret lovers' meeting between Beth and Lovett's characters could take place.

Beth shook her head. It all seemed so simple on the page…

"Your line in this scene is 'Who goes there?'" she told Lucy. "Are you quite comfortable with that?"

"It is only one line!" Lucy protested. "How am I supposed to embrace my character with only a single line of dialogue?"

"You do have several other lines later in the play," Huntingdon pointed out, with a level of patience Beth

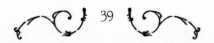

had to admire. "Can we just focus on rehearsing this scene, please, ladies?"

Lady Lucy glared down from her canvas-and-timber turret. "This window is too small!"

"I beg your pardon?"

"The window. It does not display my shoulders to their best advantage!" Lucy stood up and angrily climbed back down the ladder. "I refuse to perform unless I can be properly seen. Have your carpenter enlarge it! Within the hour!"

Once Lucy had left the hall, Huntingdon sighed heavily and covered his face with his hand. "We may as well take an early lunch break. Off you go, everybody."

One dispirited lunch break later, Beth returned to the hall. Prentice Kipps had enlarged the window and Lucy had already taken her place behind it, looking smug.

"At last! She's here!" Lucy said, rolling her eyes as she saw Beth come in. "Now perhaps we can begin?"

Beth wasn't late and everyone knew it, but she bit her tongue and apologized for her tardiness anyway. She saw Wilmot's face in her memory and heard him repeat the words "It is very important that young Lady Lucy be kept happy…"

"King and country," she whispered to herself,

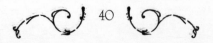

clenching her fists.

"Very good," Huntingdon said to the gathered company, clapping his hands together. "Let's begin. Beth, when you're ready."

Beth began to tiptoe across the polished wooden floor, which was standing in for the palace garden. Lucy pretended to see her, gave an exaggerated gasp, leaned over the edge of her window and called "Who *goes* there?"

Lovett was ready. "Hush, hush, sweet sister, 'tis but the wind you hear," he said. "Away to bed again, and rest your soul—"

"Stop!" Lucy ordered him. "Master Huntingdon, I wish to start the scene again."

"Oh … very well," Huntingdon said. "Places, everyone. Beth, when you're ready."

Once more, Beth tiptoed across the floor. Once more, Lucy made her startled appearance at the window, popping up like a jack-in-the-box. This time, she boomed "Who goes *there*?"

"*Hush, hush, sweet sister—*" Lovett tried to say, but again Lucy interrupted him.

"Master Huntingdon, I require your opinion. Which is the better? 'Who goes *there*?' or 'who *goes* there?'"

Beth could feel the irritation radiating from the other cast members. They were standing back, arms folded or thrust into their pockets, glaring at Lucy.

"It's a minor line," Huntingdon tried to assure her. "All you have to do is say it, then Lovett and Beth can continue the scene."

"A *minor* line?" Lucy bristled. "It introduces the character of the princess! Her first words should declare her innermost soul to the audience!"

Beth and Lovett could only watch, helpless to intervene, as Lucy dragged Huntingdon into a numbingly tedious discussion about the scene. When Lucy had finally been placated, they started the scene over again. And again. After three more false starts, with Lucy changing the inflection each time and wanting to discuss it to death, Beth was about ready to start hurling the rotten eggs herself.

Huntingdon was clearly feeling the pressure too. "Would you please just *say the line*, Lady Lucy," he said through clenched teeth. "Other members of this cast do have lines to practise too!"

"In the German Royal Court, it was considered an honour to act alongside me," Lucy sniffed. "Your players should be grateful I am giving them that same honour."

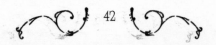

Beth tried to contain her sigh. They might be safe from the plague here, she thought wearily, but having Lady Lucy dumped on them was a whole new kind of ordeal. Not only was her lack of professional stage experience embarrassing and obvious, but she also seemed to think everyone ought to be in awe of her royal connections as she ordered the cast around like flunkies. They were enduring it well, thank goodness; like Beth they were professionals, even if they didn't also have the added responsibility of being a spy working to protect the King...

Jake, another of the actors, had even tried to butter Lucy up by flattering her, talking about her noble relatives and what an honour it would be for the company to give the first night's performance in the King's presence. The look of cold contempt Lucy had given him in response would have frozen the Thames. As Beth thought over that nasty moment, she began to wonder. Had Lucy's sneer been meant for Jake, or did she feel disdain of some sort for her cousin, King Charles?

As the long afternoon of rehearsals limped towards its end, Beth was given yet another reason to be angry with Lucy. When Beth was in the middle of her first speech, a merry one about how sweet and full of secret

promise the palace gardens were after dark, the younger girl suddenly cut her off mid-flow.

"Master Huntingdon!" Lady Lucy declared. "I have a most splendid suggestion!"

"Yes?" Huntingdon said wearily.

"Surely it is I, the princess, who should be speaking these lines? These royal gardens are mine, are they not?"

Maisie, watching from the audience, looked on in disbelief, her mouth gaping wide enough to catch flies. Beth clenched her fingers tight and told herself to keep calm.

Huntingdon was helpless to object. "I suppose we could try the scene that way, if Beth doesn't mind?"

Lucy gave Beth a venomous glance, as if she were daring her to object.

"Master Huntingdon is our director, Lady Lucy," Beth said sweetly. "A good actress must always listen to what her director tells her to do."

Lucy completely missed the rebuke in Beth's words and just smiled primly. A short while later, when only Beth could hear, she leaned over and whispered, "Master Huntingdon will not always be your director, you know."

"I'm sure I don't know what you mean," said Beth, trying to contain her frown.

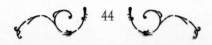

"I have friends all over London," Lucy said with a smile that cracked her thick make-up like rotting plaster. "Soon *I* will be the one directing you. Just you see."

Beth took a deep breath and gave Lucy her very broadest smile. "Won't that be fun?"

By the end of the day, Lucy had persuaded Huntingdon to transfer half a page's worth of Beth's lines to herself. Beth held it in until she reached her room, then threw herself on the bed with a cry of sheer exasperation.

"I knew she was a bad 'un!" Maisie said angrily. "I wouldn't stand for it."

"I don't suppose it's her fault, really," Beth said. "She's just spoiled rotten. She wants everything her own way. They must have treated her like a precious little princess over in the German court!"

Maisie stood firm. "You should complain to Master Huntingdon about it, miss! I don't know why he lets her get away with it!"

I do, Beth thought to herself. *He has no choice. It's all part of this diplomatic chess game…*

Losing some of her lines to another actress wasn't so bad. She could deal with that. But the way Lucy mangled their delivery? That was more than Beth could bear. She groaned and rolled over face down onto the

pillow, stifling the angry words that might have come out of her mouth.

Lady Lucy Joseph was right about one thing, though – Huntingdon wouldn't always be her director, but not because he'd lose his job. Beth had always dreamed of being in charge of a troupe of her own. She held onto that thought, imagining the productions she'd put on, the bold decisions she'd make – not only as an actress but as an undercover spy too. Dynamic and daring, loved, without others knowing her alternate occupation…

Someone was tramping up the stairs, interrupting Beth's reverie. A folded piece of paper was thrust under the door. "Letter for Miss Johnson," the innkeeper's gruff voice declared. She sprang across the room and snatched it up. The return address proclaimed it to be from a Mr Aleister Edwards of Wardour Street, London.

Beth fought to hide her excitement from Maisie's eager gaze. "Uh, it's from one of my gentleman admirers," she said. "Nothing interesting, I'm afraid."

Once Maisie was out of the room, Beth quickly broke the seal on the letter and unfolded it. Cramped handwriting filled the page:

My dear cousin Beth,

It is many days since last we met, and this dreadful plague has taken its toll on many of our neighbours. I fear that unless some relief is found...

And so on and so forth.

Beth squinted and crossed the room to the window to hold the paper up to the light. Shining through the paper, so tiny you could barely see them at all, were pinpricks. They marked the letters Beth was truly meant to read among all the filler. The C and O of the word "cousin", the M of "many", the E of "since"…

It took Beth only a minute to decipher the *real* message – from her spymaster Alan Strange:

*Come London urgent. Bell tower.
Letter is yr cover. S.*

The letter mentioned how gravely ill Beth's old friend Mr Collins was. She of course had no friend called Mr Collins, any more than she had an admirer called Aleister. That had to be what Strange meant by "cover". Heart pounding at the thought of a new assignment, Beth went

to find Huntingdon immediately. It was almost a relief to be leaving, she thought as she descended the stairs. Even if London were full of plague, at least a certain enthusiastic amateur wouldn't be there!

She knew however, with a twist in her heart, that Maisie *would* be difficult to leave – and would be very apprehensive about her friend returning to London. But Huntingdon took it surprisingly well.

"Of course you must go," he said. "I pray it's not the plague he has. May God be merciful."

"Amen," Beth said meekly.

"However, no matter what else happens, promise me you will return for the opening night," said Huntingdon pointedly. "If you don't, well … I will have no choice but to give your part to Lady Lucy Joseph…"

Chapter Four

A New Assignment

"Were you followed here?"

"No, I don't think so," Beth said, caught momentarily off guard.

"That's not good enough," Alan Strange snapped. "Don't waste my time with guesswork. You must be certain."

Beth made a mental note never to give vague answers to Strange in the future. The spymaster was as exact as a surgeon's knife, and when he needed to be, just as deadly.

She stood at the very top of the Bell Tower of St Paul's Cathedral. Strange was standing opposite her, closer to the ledge, unconcerned by the dizzying drop down to the streets below – as it was their regular meeting place, he'd clearly become accustomed to it. Wrapped in his heavy cloak even on this suffocatingly hot day, he reminded Beth of a roosting bat.

Anxious to prove herself, Beth recounted her journey. "I went in through the front door of Mrs Conway's haberdashery and left by the back, into the alley. There weren't any other customers. I doubled back when I got to Tanner's Lane. I only heard my own footsteps in the hallway downstairs, and they're marble tiles, so nobody could have crossed them without me hearing the sound of their shoes. If anyone was following me, I lost them long before I reached here."

"Someone walking barefoot, or in stockinged feet, would make no noise even on marble," Strange reminded her. "Be wary of making assumptions, Beth. They can get you killed."

"I'm sorry, sir." She sighed. "I'll be more careful in future."

"Good. Now, you'll be wondering why I summoned you. I'll come straight to it. There is a new plot on the King's life." Strange looked down at Beth, meeting her eye for the first time. She saw the weariness of many

sleepless nights in that bloodshot stare. "We knew this would happen, of course. Cut one head off and two grow in its place. It was only ever a matter of time before these King-killers began to plot again."

"What do we know?" she asked, her breathing quickening in spite of herself. "Is it Groby? Or … Vale?" Beth thought back to the conspirators whose plot they had foiled not so long ago – Edmund Groby, a menacing thug with one finger missing. And he reported, they believed, to Sir Henry Vale – the shadowy figure who had plotted against the King but somehow faked his own execution…

"Thus far we know next to nothing for certain," Strange said gravely. "Whispers, rumours, stories of cloaked figures in the dark, yet no confirmation of who could be behind the plot. But there's surely some fire causing all the smoke. We've got our hands on what could be the first piece of solid evidence."

"But you're not *certain* of the plot," Beth said, her brow knitting.

"No," Strange admitted, flinching in frustration at the word. "The evidence we have is not much, I grant you. Nothing but a single scrap of paper that happened to cost a man his life. And if it turns out to be worthless,

then I'll have that on my conscience 'til my dying day."

Beth raised an eyebrow. "Would the King's enemies really kill a man over something worthless?"

"Right now in London, life is cheap," Strange retorted. "Bodies lie in the streets; men stab each other over the price of a half pint of watered beer. But if there is any worth to this scrap of paper, Beth, I need you to find it out."

"I promise I'll do my utmost," she said, standing taller automatically.

"I expect no less."

"But…"

"You're wondering why I asked *you*," Strange said. "What's the matter? Losing confidence, are you? Want to go back to amateur work?"

Beth shook her head hastily. "I'm no amateur," she said, choosing her words carefully. Strange hated false modesty even more than he hated imprecision. "But I'm not stupid either, sir. I know I'm not your most experienced. And if I were in your shoes, with the King's life at stake, I'd send my very best."

"As would I, on any other day," Strange said. "But the plague has cost us dearly. Many of my best spies are dead now from this damned disease. Men who've survived

stab wounds in Italy and poison in France, now dead like dogs, left unburied in the streets of the country they fought to protect." He shook his head. "I'm pitching you into deep waters, girl. I know that. But you have already succeeded in foiling one such plot—"

"And I'm not a child playing at rogues-and-rascals, Master Strange," Beth said quickly. "I know the work we do is dangerous."

Strange gave a single nod of agreement. "And of course," he continued, "as a woman, you'll arouse less suspicion."

Beth smiled. "That's what you said on the first day I met you, sir. 'If people don't believe women can be spies, they might not see one even if she's right under their nose.'"

Strange did not return her smile, though she saw his eyes twinkle a little in the gloom of the tower. "Go to 19 Threadneedle Street in Bishopsgate," he said. "The next stage of your briefing will take place there."

Beth didn't need to write the address down. She had always been brilliant at remembering spoken words. It was part of what made her such an accomplished actress – and a promising spy.

"Be careful, Beth," Strange warned as she turned to

leave. "A spy has already died observing these people, remember. Let your guard down, even for a second, and they'll kill you too."

As Beth walked through the London streets towards Bishopsgate, she barely recognized the city. The big shops and boutiques that she had loved to dawdle in front of were shuttered up. Hastily scrawled notices told of how the shopkeepers had left for the cleaner air of the country and assured the customers that all would return to normal once the plague had passed. Beth wondered if they really believed London would ever be normal again.

As she passed through the poorer districts, she entered a vision of hell beyond anything Dante or Virgil could have conjured. She was unsure why, but fires were burning on the street corners, sending clouds of smoke up into the air. Figures shuffled back and forth on the streets, wearing grey rags, groaning aloud. Beth held her head high as she walked into the terrible scene, willing herself not to believe that these were London's last days. The hot stench of the smoke burned her nose and throat, and it wasn't just wood smoke, she realized. There were

spices, the malty smell of hops, the thick head-spinning perfume of frankincense. Passing by one bonfire, she saw grim-faced men throwing fresh handfuls of pepper on the flames. A sudden stab of pungent smoke made her eyes water and she sneezed violently.

"God bless you, miss," said one of the men, crossing himself as he did so.

"What are you doing?" Beth asked, finally allowing curiosity to get the better of her.

"Purifying the air, miss," the man said. "Orders of His Majesty's Government."

"We'd do better to burn the poxy houses if you ask me," his companion said, and spat.

"Plague's borne on the air," the first man said, ignoring him. "So we burn strong-smelling stuff, to turn the plague away. You should carry a posy, miss. Have you not got one?"

"Uh, I left it back at my lodgings," Beth lied.

The man passed her a fistful of small, crumpled flowers. Beth stammered her thanks and turned to leave, her eyes watering from the peppery smoke. Near the end of the street, something loomed at her out of the smoke – it looked like a raven-headed monster wearing a long coat and carrying a rod. With an involuntary gasp, she

backed away from the apparition as it slowly turned to face her. As she gaped at it, Beth realized that the head of the creature was actually a leather mask. The huge eyes above the beaklike nose were lenses. Suddenly, Beth remembered hearing about such practices.

"A-are you a plague doctor?" she stammered.

The figure nodded, and to Beth's amazement, gave a formal bow, then went on its way. Beth stared after it, her heart pounding. She remembered Maisie's terrified description of these plague doctors, self-appointed experts who roamed the streets of London looking for victims to cure – though the cures were often quack medicine that did the sufferers more harm than good. They wore long coats to keep the "bad air" away, and wore masks for the same reason. The huge beaks, which looked so frightening, were full of herbs – hyssop and rue and lavender – to purify the air the doctors breathed.

Beth hurried on before any more grotesque figures could emerge from the smoke and shadows.

"Hell is empty," she said to herself, quoting Shakespeare, "and all the devils are here…"

In spite of her hopes, the scenes of horror did not lessen as she passed further into the bowels of London – if anything, they grew even worse. As she walked past

the churchyard of St Botolph, she saw a gigantic muddy-walled hole had been dug. White, motionless human bodies lay inside it, their mouths open to the London clay, their stiff limbs sprawled higgledy-piggledy. There were hundreds of them. Beth bit down on her knuckle to keep a surge of nausea from overwhelming her. As she watched, a gravedigger hauled a cart up to the pit's edge and dumped a fresh load of bodies in. They went tumbling down with a horrible sound of sliding and rustling. Once, these people had names. They had families, trades, memories and dreams. Now, bundled together in death, they were nothing but flesh...

The gravedigger looked up and saw the expression on her face. "At least we're burying 'em, miss!" he protested. "They'd lie in the streets otherwise!"

"I'm sorry," Beth said. "But ... can't it be done some other way? This seems so inhuman. Burying them all together like rubbish."

"It ain't pretty, but it's got to be done," the gravedigger replied. "There's no room, that's the trouble. More dead than the parish can find graves for."

Beth forced herself to look down into the pit again. Death didn't play favourites, she saw. Old and young alike were piled up like carcasses in a slaughterhouse. She

sighed and started to move on, and when the gravedigger noticed she was leaving, he called after her: "God save the King!"

"God save the King," she gratefully said back to him, picking up speed as she walked. *Yes*, she thought. *London, and all of England, needs the King now more than ever.* That gravedigger understood – he had seen more of death and horror than anyone, and yet he still did his duty, because it needed to be done. Because duty and loyalty were important. Determination rose in her as she strode through the streets. *He's doing his duty*, she thought. *I shall do mine. We'll need a strong and healthy King in charge to guide us out of this darkness, and it's my duty to keep him safe from harm…*

Finally, Beth arrived at the house in Threadneedle Street, and despite the horrors of her journey, she'd kept her mind on her spycraft and had watched for figures shadowing her. She was entirely certain this time that she hadn't been followed. The street was empty but for her.

She stood at the door, about to knock, but was startled as she noticed two familiar faces watching her through the window.

Chapter Five

Mors Ad Regi

As Beth saw who was waiting inside at the address Strange had sent her to, a sudden rush of emotions went through her: surprise, delight, excitement. On the other side of the glass, she saw Ralph and John look at one another and grin, beckoning her to come in.

"It's so good to see you again! Where have you been?" John Turner exclaimed, clearly overjoyed to see her. He seemed for a moment as though he was going to take her in his arms and hug her like a gallant hero, but instead he took her hand awkwardly and then let it go again with a lopsided smile. Beth returned it warmly. It was good to see

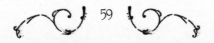

her friends and fellow spies again – they'd had a handful of smaller assignments from Strange over the past few months, but lately it had been almost ominously quiet on that front. And when they weren't working, Strange had advised them not to spend too much time in one another's company, lest their cover be blown. Still, in spite of not seeing each other often, the three of them had grown close, and now had a strong bond that Beth held dear.

"I've been in Oxford!" Beth replied. "It's a long story. I'll tell you when we have more time."

"How's your health?" John asked hesitantly. "You've been well, I hope?"

"Huntingdon says I'm blooming like a spring rose," Beth laughed.

Ralph Chandler chuckled. "Use your eyes, John! Does she look like she's had the plague?"

"It doesn't hurt to ask," John muttered.

"Well, I see you two are both fine and healthy!" Beth said. "Thank goodness. And your sister, John? How's Polly?"

"She's well," John said. "As well as she can be, I mean. She's being looked after."

Beth understood. Polly had two withered legs and couldn't walk without help – if John had thought she was

in the slightest danger, he wouldn't have left her side. After the horrors of her walk over, Beth was suddenly feeling as light as a dandelion seed. John and Ralph were safe. None of them had the plague. Sweet relief washed over her.

"I tried to find you," John continued breathlessly, "but I didn't know where to start. The plague is just everywhere, and at first Strange wouldn't help at all…"

"You know why he wouldn't as well as I do," Ralph put in. "We're not meant to spend too much time together unless we're working on a case. You never know who's watching."

Beth noticed Ralph was still dressed in the same grubby clothes he'd been wearing when she first met him. *Knowing him, he probably sleeps in them too*, she thought fondly.

"Well, we're working on a case now, so let's make the most of it!" she said with a smile. "Strange said you would brief me on what we've found out so far."

Ralph jerked his thumb towards the back of the little house. "Papers are all on the kitchen table."

"Strange said a spy was killed?" Beth said, as John led the way through to the kitchen. It was drab and functional, completely cheerless. No pictures on the walls, not even so much as a looking glass, she observed. This was clearly not

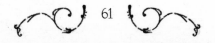

a house where anyone stayed for very long.

Ralph nodded. "Jeffrey Tynesdale. "He was good – one of Strange's best. Nobody expected *him* to get offed. It fair rattled old Strange when Tynesdale got his skull split."

Beth pursed her lips disapprovingly, and began to study the papers spread out on the table.

"Can I fetch you some water, Beth? You must be parched!" John said. He flushed a little. "I mean, I'm getting some for myself anyway, so—"

"I've got something better than water," Ralph interjected proudly. He rummaged in a sack and set three dark bottles down on the table. Each one was stoppered with a cork and sealed with a blob of scarlet wax. "It's medicine," he said, seeing the dubious looks on John and Beth's faces. "What did you think it was, liquor?"

"I wouldn't put it past you," John retorted.

Ralph rolled his eyes at them both. "Not when I'm on a job for Strange. This is a herbal infusion. Culpeper says there's nothing better for protection against the plague."

Of course, Beth thought. Ralph's landlord was a master herbalist by the name of Walter Culpeper, and he had seemed to know what he was talking about from her brief encounter with him all those months ago. She twisted

the stopper from her bottle and sniffed. A powerful acrid scent like burning phosphorus left her nose tingling. *This will not be pleasant*, she thought.

"We should have a toast," she said brightly, holding her bottle up.

"What shall we drink to?" John said, opening his own and grimacing as the smell hit his nose.

Ralph stood. "Here's a health to His Majesty, blessings on our enterprise, and swift ruin to all England's enemies!"

"And good fortune to our ships at sea," John added.

"Right. The ships an' all."

"I'll drink to that!" Beth said with a laugh.

The bottles clinked and they drank the potion down.

"Blimey," Ralph said with a cough. He shook his head like a soaking wet dog that had just jumped out of the river. "There's potent."

"Hate to seem ungrateful," John choked out, "but are you sure that wasn't *poison*?"

Beth couldn't speak. The liquid had burned like fire going down, and now it lay in her stomach like a bar of hot iron. Her mouth was full of the taste of burdock and honey, with the smell of musty cellars. She prayed it was true that strong herbs repelled the plague, because if they didn't, she was suffering through this for nothing. When

she finally managed to talk again, she laid a hand on John's arm.

"Actually … I think I'd like some water after all, please!"

They spent the next hour sitting around the kitchen table, sorting through the notes that Strange had left them. One crucial scrap of paper sat in the midst of all the others; the evidence Strange had mentioned – the one that had cost Jeffrey Tynesdale his life. Beth yearned to look at it, but John told her Strange had said to go over the other documents first. Many of those were letters written by Tynesdale to Strange, laying out the course of his investigation in painstaking detail. John read the letters aloud while Ralph and Beth listened carefully.

It seemed Tynesdale had followed a trail of rumours across the city to the Four Swans tavern in Bishopsgate, only three streets away from where they sat now. He'd begun to visit the inn regularly, blending in like the professional he was, drawing no attention to himself. He spoke little and listened much.

His main target was a man called Martin Sykes. "'I am

becoming certain the man is a King-killer conspirator,'" John read. "'When drunk, he talks much of the King's failings – as he supposes them to be – to any who will listen, and though he speaks no treason openly, he glares about himself with such dark looks that I am sure he yearns to.'"

By the sound of it, eventually Tynesdale's patience had paid off. By chance he overheard a conversation, "the voices too low for me to tell who spoke," mentioning that Martin Sykes had been entrusted to bring a message to someone that night. Tynesdale knew then that he had to intercept that message and bring it to Strange at all costs.

"So how did Tynesdale die?" Beth asked.

"Coshed over the back of the head, not a stone's throw from his own front door," said Ralph. "We're just lucky he got the paper to Strange first."

"Do you think it was Sykes who killed him?"

"Seems likely. Once he found out the paper was gone, he'd have known something was up."

"He must have lain in wait near Tynesdale's house, knowing he would come back eventually," John said. "Which means he knew where Tynesdale lived…"

"Someone was watching *him*, while he was watching

them," Beth said with a shudder. She reached for the scrap of paper. "Come on, boys. Let's see what Sykes might have been willing to kill for."

She unfolded the paper and smoothed it out on the table. All three of them craned in close to see what it said.

Down the centre of the paper ran a list of initials:

Below the letters was a strange pictogram. In the centre were two concentric rings, like the letter O within a larger O, and underneath that was a crude drawing of a lion's head facing forward. Above the circles was an image that looked like a bridge in three parts, below which lay a wavy line.

At the very bottom of the paper were three words, all in capitals.

"*Mors ad Regi*," John read aloud.

They all stared in silence for a long time.

Ralph was the first to speak. "What's that supposed to mean? Don't even sound like English."

Beth didn't recognize it either. "Maybe it's a name?" she guessed.

Ralph slapped the table. "'Course it is. Must be two names, not one!" he exclaimed. "Morse and Reggie. They must be two of the men behind all this!"

Beth frowned, unsure, but she noticed John had turned pale. "Neither of you ever studied Latin, did you?" he asked quietly.

"What do you think?" Ralph scoffed. "Latin, indeed!"

"I was always too busy with the stage," Beth said. "But you do have some Latin, don't you, John?"

"You pick it up, doing the clerical work I do." John rubbed his forehead. "It's not a name at all. '*Mors*' means 'death', and '*ad Regi*' means 'unto the King'."

Beth swallowed hard – it was just what they had been dreading.

"Death to the King…"

Chapter Six

A Piece of the Puzzle

"Well, that they're King-killers is not a great surprise, I suppose," Ralph said with a sigh. "But what about these initials, and the drawings?"

"I'd guess that the initials must stand for names," Beth said. "This could be a list of people?"

"Makes sense," Ralph agreed. "But who? Conspirators? Or people they wanted to get rid of?"

"There's no 'MS' on the list," John pointed out. "If it was the conspirators, wouldn't Martin Sykes be down there too?"

"Not if he was only the message-bearer," Beth said. "If

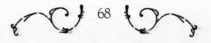

it were the conspirators themselves, whoever wrote this wouldn't write their whole names down. If it fell into the wrong hands, it would prove their guilt."

"That still doesn't make sense," John complained. "The conspirators must know who they are, surely? They wouldn't need a note to tell them. So why write down a list of their initials?"

John's argument was sound, but Beth still couldn't shake the feeling that the initials represented the conspirators somehow. Something about that list – the style of it – was oddly familiar. Whoever had sent the message wasn't just passing information – they were giving an order. Perhaps confirming some sort of arrangement?

Beth murmured to herself, reading down the list again. "Mister S.P., Mister L.B., who could you be…? Wait! That's it!" She snapped her fingers. "I knew it reminded me of something!"

"Go on," John urged her.

"It's like the way the *Gazette* reports the billing for our plays," she said. "Little narrow columns down the page. Mister F.D. as Julius Caesar, Miss B.J. as Cleopatra."

"You think this is a cast list, Beth?" Ralph said, looking at her incredulously.

"Of course not," she said with a grin. "But it's *like* one. It's like how the director chooses the cast for the play. I think whoever sent this is telling the conspirators who he's chosen to play the parts in his plot!"

"I see what you mean," John said eagerly. "They could be saying, 'These are the people I've picked to do the job.'"

"Exactly," Beth said, feeling like a piece of the puzzle had clicked into place. She wished Strange could see her working like this. She may not have been his most experienced spy, but she was certainly no amateur!

"I dunno," said Ralph, leaning back in his chair and folding his arms. "Seems like a bit of a wild guess to me … Meaning no disrespect, of course, Beth."

John tutted at his reclining friend. "At least it's a start," he said, then turned back to look at the paper. "What about the rest of it, though? The circle inside a circle, and some sort of bridge, a wavy line and a lion's head? I suppose it's some kind of code, but I haven't a clue what it could mean."

"Well, if the first part is picking out the people for the job," Beth said, "maybe the second part is telling them what the job actually is?"

"'Death to the King,'" Ralph quoted. "That's got to

be the job, ain't it? Killing the King."

"There's got to be more detail here than that," Beth insisted. "They wouldn't just tell the conspirators to go and kill the King. That's not much of a plot."

"It's about the only part of this ruddy thing that we *do* know," muttered Ralph, then he straightened up. "I reckon that lion's head means the same thing. Lions are symbols of kings, aren't they?"

"There's three lions on the King's banner," John pointed out.

"Right!" said Ralph enthusiastically. "And what happens if you chop a lion's head off? It dies, don't it?"

"I imagine so," John said, hiding a smile. "I've never had the chance to find out."

Ralph continued, oblivious. "There you go, then. Lion's head means 'Death to the King'. Simple. No need to make it any more complicated than it already is."

"Well, one thing's obvious," John said, standing up. "We need to act, and act *now*. The King's life is at stake."

"Now you're talking sense," Ralph said, on his feet in a second. "Come on."

John raised an eyebrow. "Where to?"

"We should pick up where Jeffrey Tynesdale left off. The Four Swans tavern. That's where Martin Sykes was

71

drinking when Jeffrey lifted the note off him, wasn't it?"

"Good idea. It's about the only lead we have. Beth?" John held Beth's cloak out to her expectantly, but she remained seated.

"Wait. We're not finished." She pointed at the circles, the bridge and the wavy line. "We haven't accounted for these symbols yet. They must mean *something*."

"Surely we can think about that later?"

"He's right!" said Ralph irritably. "Come on, Beth, we could stare at that scrap of paper all night and be none the wiser. In the meantime, in case you hadn't noticed, there's a plot being hatched out there."

"And this piece of paper is our only clue to what exactly it is!" she retorted. "Strange wanted us to look into it. Do you want to go back to him and apologize, saying we didn't think it necessary to unravel every clue we could?" She finally stood and accepted her cloak from John. "We can go to the Four Swans later. There's one other place I want to go first. Derby Place."

"The College of Arms?" John said in disbelief. Seeing Ralph's baffled face, he explained. "It's where the heralds are based. They're the officials who handle coats of arms, rights to noble titles and that kind of thing, on the government's behalf."

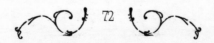

72

Ralph raised an eyebrow. "Heraldry, eh?"

"I think these look like heraldic symbols," Beth said. "I'm sure I've seen them before."

"So, what do you imagine, you're just going to march up to a building full of high and mighty officials who deal with lords and earls, and ask for a natter over a glass of brandy?" Ralph looked deeply cynical. "Pardon me for a moment while I pop 'ome and put on my best Sunday wig!"

"I have a friend in the college," Beth said. Both of them looked stunned at that, and she allowed herself a moment of pleasure at their surprise.

"A friend?" John asked, and Beth thought she heard a hint of jealousy in his voice. "You think he can help?"

"It's got to be worth a try."

John sucked air through his teeth. "I think we're going to have to let Beth try there first, Ralph."

The other spread his hands. "Fine, fine. I know when I'm beat."

Beth gave them both an enigmatic smile. "Then it's settled, boys. I'm going to go and see the Red Dragon…"

* * *

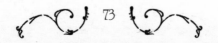

The three of them hurried through the streets, with Beth making sure to keep a good distance from the boys, so they weren't obviously together. As spies, they could blow their cover if anyone made a connection between the three of them, but by now they were used to this covert way of moving through the streets and talking without seeming to be together. The paper, folded up into a tight wad, lay at the bottom of Beth's purse.

"So how do you know this friend of yours at the college?" John asked, a little too casually, as he brushed past her. Beth fought to keep amusement from showing on her face.

"He's a regular at the theatre," she murmured back as John paused, pretending to adjust his boot a few paces later. "Francis Sandford. He's a charming old gentleman, and he simply *loves* to talk about symbols and heraldry. He has books full of them." She shook her head, thinking about how Sandford loved to talk her ear off about the subject when he came backstage to praise her performances.

"Thought you said you were off to see a red dragon?" said Ralph, feigning to cough to cover his speech as he passed a group of ladies.

"That's his title. Rouge Dragon Pursuivant. All the

heralds have titles like that. Bluemantle, Garter Principal, Unicorn. It's like the Knights of the Round Table."

Beth could see Ralph roll his eyes as she glanced over at him, but she ignored him.

"Who's the head of the College of Arms?" John wondered aloud.

"I believe it's Lord Beaumont, the Duke of Norfolk…"

Finally they reached the grand mansion house close to the north bank of the Thames, and Derby Place, the headquarters of the College of Arms, loomed up at them. "Right, you both should stay out here while I go in. It shouldn't take me too long."

Ralph and John both nodded and moved away from the entrance to wait for her. Beth spoke to the officer on duty beside the gate, which was a heavy wood-and-iron portcullis like a castle might have. After some eyelash batting, the guard smiled and admitted her.

She crossed the quadrangle and passed through the inner doors. White-wigged scholars were going to and fro inside, and heads turned to watch her wherever she went. Beth just marched ahead as if she had a perfect right to be there, but wrinkled her nose at the musty, cloistered smell of the place. *Like a crypt*, she thought. *Or the castle of some mad baron from old times.* The coats

of arms hanging on the walls blazed with bright colours against the dark oak panelling. She climbed the stairs to the upper hallway where a door stood ajar. A mist of smoke was drifting from it.

A quick knock brought a croak of, "Come in, Miss Johnson!" from inside.

"How did you know it was me?" she laughed, as she swept into the room.

"A lovely young woman, entering this nest of ancient ravens?" The man behind the desk could barely be seen through clouds of tobacco smoke. "That's a major piece of news, my dear. Whispers travel swiftly in a place like this." He leaned forward through the clouds, long clay pipe in one hand, open book in the other. His milky eyes still glittered with intelligence. "Now, to what do I owe the pleasure?"

"It's something of an usual request, but I was hoping you could look at some symbols for me," Beth said. "If you have pen and paper, I'll draw them."

Francis Sandford sucked deeply on his pipe and blew a long column of smoke up at the ceiling. Beth couldn't help thinking that whoever had given him the title of Rouge Dragon Pursuivant must have had a sense of humour.

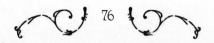

"I'd be overjoyed to. Anything for you, Miss Johnson," he said. "Draw your symbols, please. The more obscure, the better!" He passed her a quill and paper. "One gets so very bored of tracking down the rights to extinct titles for upstart little lords…"

When Beth had finished, he took the paper in a claw-like hand and peered at it. A deep rumble came from his throat – the sound she knew he always made when he was thinking deeply.

"Hmm … this is most irregular," he said. "Lions are frequently found in heraldry." He paused, raising an eyebrow. "But they're usually displayed *rampant*, which means rearing up, or *passant*, which means walking. To have a lion *cabossed affronté* – just the head, facing forwards – is not at all common. Are you certain this is correct?"

"Yes, I'm certain. So it's not heraldic?" Beth asked.

"It may be, it may not. As for these circles, they are assuredly not. They may stand for an archery target, perhaps, or a shield boss, but you will not find them in any of the volumes on *these* shelves." He sucked on his pipe again. "But tell me, Miss Johnson, how is *Love's Green Garlands* faring? Playing to packed houses, I'll warrant…"

He obviously hadn't made it to the opening performance, Beth thought. "We're rehearsing every single day!" she said. Well, it wasn't entirely a lie – more of a half-truth. Before Sandford could draw her any further on to the subject of her acting, which would easily consume a whole hour, she asked "Uh, and what about the bridge, and this line?"

"Oh, that's straightforward enough," he said with a wave of his wet pipe stem. "Not worth bothering with really…" He paused and looked at her studiously, seeming to regard her in a new light. "It occurs to me that you've not told me where you found these peculiar symbols."

Beth's heart was suddenly pounding like a military drum. "They were written in an old book. Silly of me, I thought they might be clues to a treasure hoard or something!" She smiled in what she hoped would be a distracting fashion.

"A treasure hoard?" Sandford arched one greying eyebrow. "What a romantic notion…"

"Well, you never know!" Beth said coyly. "What do these ones mean?"

"Wavy lines usually denote water," he said after some thought, "and the symbol like a bridge indicates a First

 78

Son. I don't suppose you brought the book with you? Perhaps I could take a look—"

"I'll bring it next time," she promised quickly. All Beth wanted to do now was leave – the hair at the nape of her neck was prickling. The fact that Sandford had considered that particular symbol so "dull" had set her mind alight with suspicion and apprehension.

There was one person she knew of who used symbolism and heraldry in his cryptic messages. Someone who had crossed their path before. Not just a traitor and a King-killer, but the spider at the heart of their web. A man who she knew was a First Son.

Beth's mind silently formed the man's name, and it chilled her blood.

Sir Henry Vale.

Chapter Seven

The Four Swans

Beth quickly made her excuses and rushed out of the College of Arms. The Rouge Dragon Pursuivant's final words rang in her ears as she hurried through the double doors and out into the quadrangle: "Do be careful out there, my dear. I'd miss my favourite actress if anything happened to her…!"

It could have been a kindly warning against contracting the plague – or something more sinister. Now that the conspiracy was confirmed, Beth hardly knew who she could trust any more.

"What is it?" John hissed as he and Ralph spotted her

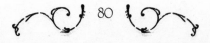

exiting the gate. The three of them paced quickly away from the building, keeping their distance.

"Not here," Beth whispered. "Wait 'til we're back on the street."

Wisely, John shut up. Beth didn't say another word until they were a good distance away from the college. Ralph led them down to the bank of the Thames, to a shadowed spot he knew down by the moorings where they could speak without being overheard. Nobody could have listened in unless they were hiding underwater, or drifting by on a passing boat.

Beth told them what she had deduced, and as soon as he heard the name Henry Vale, John visibly stiffened. They had scuppered Vale's plans once before, but it seemed as though the traitor would not give up so easily.

"Of course. The would-be King-killer himself," he whispered. "And to think I watched his execution at the Tower. Or what we all *thought* was his execution…"

"Exactly. We know Vale's lethally clever," Beth said. "Clever enough to fake something like that – and we also knew he'd rear his head again sometime soon."

John shuddered. "Rear his head indeed. I'll never forget it. For all the world it appeared that the executioner cut Vale's head clean off. The blood was like a fountain!"

81

"That just means that someone really died that day. But not Vale."

"Could have been a double," Ralph suggested. "Someone so totally, fanatically loyal that he was willing to die in Vale's place?"

It made sense, Beth thought. If anyone could talk a follower into dying in his place, Sir Henry Vale could. She recalled with horror his relentless thug Edmund Groby, with his missing finger and his willingness to stop at nothing to kill the King. "They say Vale was very persuasive," she said. "He probably *did* convince one of his people that it was his duty to die for the good of the country, ironic though that may be."

"And anyone who made that sacrifice for their cause would be remembered as a martyr," John said darkly. "How many times do you have to kill a man before he dies…?"

Beth remembered their spymaster Strange's words when she'd met him in the bell tower. *Chop off one head and two grow in its place.* Beth wondered just how much Strange had already suspected of Vale's involvement in this new plot…

"He's going to keep trying until he's stopped," she said, clenching her jaw.

"Well, we stopped him last time," John replied, sounding more optimistic now. "That's got to have set his plans back a bit. I bet we can do it again, if we move fast."

"You're right," Beth said, with a grim smile at the memory.

That adventure had ended at the side of the Thames, not far from where they stood now. With cold-blooded irony, Henry Vale had masterminded a plot to kill the King during the Bonfire Night celebrations, on the anniversary of the first Gunpowder Plot. Beth shivered as she remembered how close they had all come to death. Beth, John and Ralph had had to race against time to uncover the plot and find where the explosive had been hidden. They'd stopped the explosion just in time.

Of course, they had never seen the real Sir Henry Vale. The arch-conspirator had worked from behind the scenes, overseas, out of their reach. They only knew of his involvement because of a coded letter that Beth had found on a drifting ship. Indeed, they couldn't prove for certain that it was Vale himself and not someone using the name as a tribute – but deep in her heart Beth had been sure it was him.

"Thwarting his plot? Well, that ought to be easy,"

Ralph said with ringing sarcasm. "Now Beth's chum the old Red Dragon's cleared that note up for us, it's all as clear as crystal! Wavy lines mean water? Fan-ruddy-tastic. All we have to do now is look for a place that has water in it or near it. That narrows things down a bit!"

"If Beth hadn't stuck at it when we both wanted to rush off to the tavern, we wouldn't have cracked the *first* part of the clue! So it's lucky for us that *one* of us is so persistent." John said.

"S'pose," Ralph conceded grudgingly.

John was a little flushed now. It was charming how defensive of her he got sometimes, Beth thought with a small smile. But rather than embarrass him further, she turned her gaze out over the Thames. There was no bigger source of water in all of London. Perhaps they shouldn't overlook the obvious. And of course, there was a bridge across it, too – the famous London Bridge, spanning the waters between the City and Southwark. So many buildings had been constructed upon it that it was more of a street than a bridge. Beth remembered her first sight of the gruesome southern gatehouse, where the heads of traitors had been impaled on spikes. That horrible practice had continued for years until the King had put a stop to it.

The more Beth gazed at the river, the more certain she grew that it would play a role in their investigations. The explosive last plot had been quenched by the Thames. It seemed somehow inevitable that this one should rise back out of it...

"Well, we know a bit more about these symbols, and that's all very well," said Ralph, jolting her back to reality. "But can we *please* go to the pub now?"

"Best let me get the drinks in for us all," Ralph said as they arrived outside the Four Swans. "It'll be less conspicuous that way."

He seemed much more at home now they were at the tavern, Beth thought with some amusement.

"I know my way round an inn, thank you very much!" retorted John huffily.

"Oh, yeah? I can see yer now," Ralph grinned. "'Ho, good barkeep, a flagon of your very finest ale if you please!' You'll fit right in!"

"I'm Shadwell born and bred!" John bristled. "I may not talk the street gab like you, but I'm no toff. Watch me!"

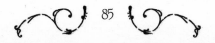

Before Beth or Ralph could protest, he'd shoved his way into the inn.

Inside, dusty beams of sunlight slanted in through the windows. Only a few drinkers sat wedged into corners or huddled around tables. The plague must be keeping them away, Beth thought. Bunches of dried-out herbs hung down from the rafters, adding their fragrant hedgerow scents to the overpowering reek of beer slops and sawdust. Her sharp eyes instantly noticed one of the tables had part of the edge broken away and the wood there was pale. Fresh damage. What had happened there?

Beth turned her attentions to John with some trepidation as he marched right up to the table where the serving woman sat. She had paid no attention to who had walked in, but when he slammed a handful of coins onto the wet surface, she finally looked up at him through narrowed eyes. Her pale, pudgy arms wobbled as she gathered the coins up. "What'll it be?"

"Jug of small ale," he grunted.

She immediately went to fill a tall jug from a barrel in the nearby taproom. There was hardly any alcohol in small ale, but it was safer to drink than water, especially these days. "Not seen you round 'ere before," she said over her shoulder.

"Wind blew me all the way from Holland," John said, with a coarse rasp in his voice that made Beth blink in surprise. "Been paid me pittance for being shot at for King and Country, and I'm looking to splash it up the wall."

He's playing the part of a sailor, Beth realized, *just back from the wars. Nicely done!* She and Ralph hung back, watching him.

"What's your ship, Jack Tar?" said the woman casually.

Panic seized Beth as she expected John to flounder. She got ready to leap in and improvise, just like she'd done so many times on the stage, but John spat on the floor and said "HMS *Fairfax*," then quietly added, "God rot her and her captain too."

The clunk of the full jug on the table top ended the conversation.

"I'll thank you for the loan of a mug," John said.

The barwoman nodded and fetched down a single tankard, which John handed to Beth as he walked over. Carrying the jug himself, he led the way to a small dark booth at the back of the inn.

"You both need something to drink out of," Beth said. "You are *not* drinking from the jug."

John and Ralph both silently unfastened leather

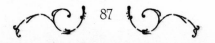 87

tankards from their belts and set them on the table. Beth realized she'd been so used to seeing them there, she'd all but forgotten what they were for.

"Fair play to you, mate," Ralph said to John, helping himself to the foaming small ale. "That went better than I'd expected."

"I know ships," John said. "I work in the Navy office, remember? You could put me in charge of one tomorrow and I'd know exactly what to do."

"Bit risky speaking ill of the Navy, though, wasn't it? I've been a powder monkey, and I've seen men flogged to the bone for talking like that."

"He spoke ill of his captain," Beth pointed out. "If this really is a pub full of Republicans, they might even admire him for it."

John nodded. "Right – time to get to work. Let's ask around the inn," he said. "What were those initials again, Beth?"

"SP, LB, JL and RM," Beth said. "You think we should ask around for names that match those?"

"If we can find a match, we've found a conspirator," John said. "Well, we might have…"

"Let's start with SP." Beth sipped her small ale, so as not to look suspicious. It wasn't particularly nice, but at

least it was safe to drink.

"It's going to be a bloke, isn't it?" said Ralph. "I mean, most villains are men."

"I'll go along with that," Beth said with a wry grin.

"So 'S' could stand for … I dunno … Simon?"

"Or Simeon?" John said. "Or Stuart. Or Sam."

"Or Sidney—" said Ralph.

"Why don't the two of you go and talk to the customers?" Beth said, interjecting. "Try to find out what their names are? I'd say that's the way to start."

"Good idea," said John.

"I'm not so sure it is," Ralph said, shaking his head. "Would you just tell your name to a total stranger who you didn't know from Adam? They'll be suspicious of people they don't know. You've got to get them off their guard."

John stood up, ignoring Ralph. "Well, I think I can do it," he said.

Ralph just raised his eyebrows and scoffed. "Fine! You go first, then."

"I will!" John slipped off to one side of the inn. Beth and Ralph listened in closely as John approached one of the drinkers.

"Sorry to bother you, gentlemen, but I'm in a rare

confusion. I'm meant to bring a message to a fellow, and dammed if I've clear forgot his name. All I recall is, he drinks here at the Four Swans."

"What *sort* of message?" asked one of the drinkers aggressively.

John scratched his head. "I'm not really at liberty to say."

"On your way, then!" the man growled.

"Whoever he is, he'll be angry when he doesn't get his three guineas," John said morosely.

At the mention of money, the men's faces changed like the sun emerging from behind a cloud. "Uh, I'm Bob Farnshaw," said the bigger one, "and this is Selwyn Tanner. Either of those ring a bell?"

"Afraid not," John said, and their faces fell again as he moved onto the next table. He seemed to be successful with his technique, customers eager to talk to him as he gave his ruse of an excuse.

"He seems to be doing quite well!" Beth said with a grin.

Ralph folded his arms. "I suppose," he sulked. "Well, I'm hopeless at that talking lark. You and silver-tongue John over there can handle that. Me, I'm 'appy with a crowbar in me hand and a locked door to crack open."

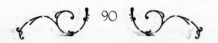

He half smiled. "Or a cove's head. That's where I'm best served. Fighting, running or climbing in and out o' things."

"That's why we're a team," Beth reassured him. "Good spies work together. We've each got our own fields of…"

Before she could finish the sentence, the plaque above the bar caught her eye:

By the Authority of His Majesty the King & the City of London, Mr Sebastian Peters is Licensed to Serve Beverages in this Place

"Ralph, look!"

He followed Beth's gaze. "Sebastian Peters," he whispered. "SP! We were so busy asking round the customers, we never thought to check the bloomin' landlord!"

Beth pencilled *Sebastian Peters?* next to the initials SP on the paper. "We need to tell John," she said. "And find this Sebastian Peters as soon as possible…"

Chapter Eight

A Close Call

John was deep in conversation with a group of four men. It took Beth several meaningful glances in his direction before he got the message and came back to their table.

"Have you found someone?" he whispered urgently.

"I think we have!" Beth said. "Look at the sign above the bar."

John did, and gave a low whistle. "No wonder this place is so bound up with the conspiracy, if the landlord himself is embroiled in it! He could be running a safe haven for every King-killer that Vale recruits!"

"Let's not judge him guilty until we've found out

more," Beth cautioned, remembering what Strange had told her about making assumptions. "John, you seem to be the most welcome of the three of us here. Can you ask the serving woman where we can find Sebastian Peters?"

"I'd better get our cover story straight just in case she takes me straight to him," John said, draining what was left of his beer. "What business might a young scallywag like me have with an innkeeper?"

"Say you're looking for work," Beth suggested. "The plague's left lots of places short-handed. You look healthy, and there's a good chance the serving woman wouldn't be able to hire anyone without the landlord's say-so."

"It's worth a try," John said, though his recent confidence seemed a little shakier now. "Wish me luck…"

All Beth and Ralph could do was watch. They couldn't hear the words that passed between John and the woman at the table, but it seemed to be taking too long for a simple conversation. Suddenly Beth felt deeply uneasy. Had all the questions John and Ralph had asked roused suspicions? If Sebastian Peters was here, why wasn't the serving woman showing John right to him?

A horrible thought occurred to her. What if *everyone* in the pub was a conspirator? There was only one door to

93

this place. It would be fatally easy for one group of men to block it off, trapping them inside while the rest of the tavern went to work on them. Everyone here could swear blind they'd never seen three young people come into the tavern. Then, many weeks later, their bodies would be fished out of the Thames…

Beth sat in a cold sweat, glancing at John from time to time, wishing he'd hurry up and come back.

"You look like you're sickenin' for something," Ralph whispered. "Are you all right? You're not … ill, are you?"

Beth shook her head. "I'm quite well. Just trying not to lose sight of the kind of people we're dealing with here."

"They're killers," Ralph agreed. "Don't you worry, though, Beth. Nobody's going to lay a finger on you. They'll have to get through me first."

That's what I'm afraid of, Beth thought. *John and I might escape to fight another day, but you're the kind of boy who'd stand and fight. That could get you killed.*

John finally turned and made his way back to their table, and Beth felt her body sagging in relief, like a puppet on suddenly slackened strings.

"What took you so long?" she whispered.

"It turns out Sebastian Peters isn't on the premises

today," John said.

Ralph swore under his breath, remembered Beth was there, and glanced at her guiltily.

"But – I do have his home address," John grinned. "It's only a few streets away. Sorry it took a long time, but Bella the serving maid didn't give it up easily. I had to pretend I'd lost half my family to the plague before she'd take pity on me."

"John, you're a marvel," Beth said, looking at him appreciatively. She felt bad for underestimating him. "Come on. Let's go and take a look."

"Why doesn't Peters live above his tavern?" Beth asked as they hurried towards the suspected conspirator's home. "Most landlords do, don't they?"

"It seems our Sebastian is something of a family man," John said. "He has too many children to cram into one room and he needs the others for paying guests, so he had to move his wife and family out into the cheapest lodgings they could find. It's Bella, that serving woman, who has the upstairs at the Four Swans."

"My mum raised six of us in one room," Ralph said

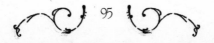

gruffly. "And it was a cellar too…"

"You're going to have to change your story, John," said Beth, ignoring their friend. "Pretending to look for work might have got Sebastian Peters down to talk to us at the pub, but it won't get us through his front door."

"You're right," John said. "Let me think…"

"Or maybe Ralph could get us in through the back door, if we went after dark," Beth suggested.

"No, wait. I've got it!" Ralph said. "Listen to this. Down at the docks, the ships are always bringing cargoes of wine in. Red wines from France and Germany, sack and brandy from Spain. The vintners buy them up from the merchants, and sell them on to the tavern keepers."

"You're going to pose as a wine merchant?" Beth said with a quizzical frown.

"Not likely," Ralph said with a wicked grin. "I'm going to pretend to be a drayman for the vintners! You see, once in a while, a barrel or two goes astray. Many's the landlord who'll happily pay for a stray barrel of wine, with no questions asked."

"You can't sell stolen wine!" John exclaimed. "Especially if it doesn't even exist!"

"Don't have to sell it," smirked Ralph. "Just need to ask if he's interested, hem and haw, haggle over the price.

 96

That should get our foot in the door."

"That could just work!" Beth said with genuine admiration. "If you can keep him talking, John and I can have a look around for clues."

Their path took them down a shadowy, narrow lane where the houses pressed in so close to each other that washing lines had been strung between the upper windows. Beth instantly felt she had to be on her guard. This was a London very far from all the bright boutiques and parlours – it was an area where the citizens had grimy faces and shoeless feet. Heads popped up at the windows to stare at them as they passed. Shutters were hastily banged to.

"Are you sure this is the way?" she asked John uncertainly.

"The street we want is at the end of this row, on the right," John assured her, though he sounded a little nervous himself.

Without warning, a group of five or six children – Beth couldn't even tell how many – came charging out of one of the houses and running up the street towards them. Mostly boys, they wore ragged shirts and breeches tied with string. A babble of half-friendly, half-aggressive shouts rained down on the three of them:

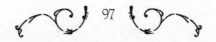

"Where you going, miss?"

"What you doing down here?"

"Spare a farthing for a poor orphan, do."

"Is he your sweetheart, miss? Is he?"

Ralph cursed as the children danced around him, pawing at his shirt, pulling at his trouser leg.

"Buy a bunch of violets, mister?"

"Here comes a chopper to chop off your head!"

Hands tugged at Beth's skirt. "Play with us. Come on. Come play with us."

"No. Be on with you. Stop it, now," Beth said through clenched teeth.

"Leave her alone!" John tried to shoulder his way between them.

Before Beth knew what was happening, her purse was snatched out of her hands, and the children all ran off in a group, tossing their prize from one to the other, laughing at the tops of their voices.

"Stop them!" she yelled.

The children were running away from the streets into the fields and brickworks to the east of Bishopsgate. Once they vanished into that barren place, they'd never be found. Beth's money was gone – but what was worse, the cipher note was gone too.

 98

Beth ran a few paces, then stopped. She couldn't hope to catch up with them. They'd lost the clue that Jeffrey Tynesdale had died to secure. Her heart sank. What would Strange say to her? *Only fit for amateur work…*

But suddenly she saw a dark figure sprinting out across the field. Beth was amazed to see it was Ralph. His reactions smart as a cracked whip, he'd taken off running after the children the instant they'd grabbed Beth's purse.

"Thank goodness!" she cried. "Get them, Ralph!"

The children fanned out across the field, each one running in a different direction. They were trying to throw him off the scent; they must be old hands at this, Beth realized. But Ralph already knew which one had the purse. Like a greyhound after a hare, he was gaining on the fleeing child. They had nearly reached the brickworks now. The boy made as if to throw the purse to his friend.

"No you don't!" Ralph roared, and flung himself at the thief. He caught him by the shirttail and both of them went down, flailing in the dust. The boy fought like a wildcat, raking at Ralph's face, and Ralph had to kneel on his chest, grab his wrists and wrench his fingers off the purse before he'd give it up. All the while, the boy kept up a loud torrent of the filthiest language Beth had ever heard.

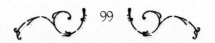

With the purse safely back in his hands, Ralph let the boy go. He was off immediately, running like a greased piglet, screaming and yelling obscenities.

"And *your* mum an' all!" Ralph yelled after him furiously. "You can tell her I said that!"

On his way back to Beth and John, Ralph traded many more shouted insults with the street children, who had retreated to the safety of the brickworks. He was limping badly when he finally pressed the purse into her hands.

"Hail, the conquering hero!" Beth said with affection. The folded paper was safe at the purse's bottom, marked with grubby fingerprints, though Beth's few coins had disappeared. "Thank you, Ralph. I don't know what I would have done if we'd lost this."

"You didn't get hurt, did you?" John asked.

Ralph shook his head, wiping away a little blood that trickled down his cheek from a scratch above the eyebrow. "Just kids mucking about," he said. "Come on. We've got work to do."

As they headed further down the cramped little lane, Beth's mind reeled at the overcrowding and sheer poverty of this district. Multiple families seemed to be living in the same house, without any fresh water or outhouses.

The stink was unbelievable. Only Ralph's quick reflexes saved John from being doused with the contents of a chamber pot, emptied out from an upstairs window. These streets were still as crowded as ever, despite the plague. London only seemed empty in the richer quarters because the people who could afford to pack up and leave had already gone, Beth realized. But nobody here had that kind of money. The families here were trapped – and the plague spread quickest where people are all pressed up together...

"Just around the corner now!" John urged.

They all started to walk a little faster, spurred on by the thought of what they might learn. *Sebastian Peters*, Beth thought. *We have a chance at apprehending our first real conspirator. He* must *know something.*

They were all rushing along so quickly, they nearly ran straight into a funeral procession.

Four young boys were carrying a coffin on their shoulders, and the tracks of their tears left white lines down through the dirt on their faces. Beth had never seen such a pitiful, boxy-looking coffin in her life. Bits of old wood were nailed crookedly together – from the look of it, it had been made of smashed-up furniture: the back of a wardrobe, the bottoms of drawers.

"Excuse me?" John asked a grave-faced man who stood watching the coffin go by. "Which one on this row is Sebastian Peters' house?"

"That's the only house Sebastian has now," the man said, pointing. "Four walls and a roof to last him 'til Judgement Day."

Ralph looked with horror to where the man was gesturing – towards the pathetic box carried on the shoulders of four young children.

We're too late, Beth thought, her heart sinking. *The plague has taken him.*

Chapter Nine

A Worrying Discovery

"Those boys carrying the coffin – are they his sons?" John asked hollowly.

The man watching the funeral procession gave a curt nod. "Four sons he had, and three girls. And a wife."

"Poor things," Beth said, her heart heavy. Whether Sebastian Peters had been a conspirator or not, these boys were mourning their father. And maybe they'd be mourning their mother too, soon enough. In houses like these, with so many families crammed in together, the plague would spread like wildfire.

"Do we talk to 'em?" said Ralph reluctantly. "They

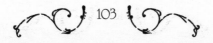

might know something."

Beth looked at the boys' tearful faces. "I doubt it. And I think their fortunes have been bitter enough already."

"That settles that," John said. "We may as well forget about being able to look around inside Peters' house too."

"Too right. I'm not going inside a plague house, not for anything," Ralph agreed. "If Strange wants to go poking around in a plague house, he can ruddy well do it himself."

"So we're back to where we started," John sighed. "Nothing but a piece of paper to go on."

"Let's go back to the Four Swans," Beth said. "Their landlord's in a coffin, and they don't even know it yet. Maybe there's still some information to be had there."

They made their way quickly and solemnly back through the streets to the tavern, but outside the pub Ralph stopped in his tracks. The drayman's trap door, which led to the tavern's cellar from the pavement outside, was open. That usually only happened when the draymen needed to drop the barrels down, but there was no sign of a delivery cart. Maybe they were late, or maybe the serving woman had forgotten to close and bolt the trap door.

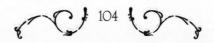

Any which way, Beth could see it was an opportunity he couldn't resist.

"You're going down there, aren't you," she said with a wry smile.

Ralph grinned. "You two go on ahead. I'm going to have a nose around – Peters might have left some clues down there."

With a quick glance back up the street to check there was nobody watching him, Ralph ducked under the window level and began to climb down through the trap door. He gripped the edge and lowered himself down until he was hanging by his arms like a monkey.

"Be careful," Beth warned.

"I'm always careful," Ralph panted. "But if I'm not back up in an hour, send out the search party…"

Beth looked at John. "Let's go and deliver the ill tidings," she said. "With any luck, they'll all be too busy mourning Peters to give any thought to what might be happening in the cellar."

They went inside and the doors swung shut behind them. John ordered more beer, and then quietly broke the news to Bella about her landlord. Word soon spread around the pub, and as the patrons began to eye the two of them curiously, Beth and John quickly moved

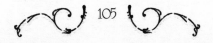

to sit together in the darkened booth again. She crossed out the name *Sebastian Peters*, that she'd pencilled on the paper.

"I'm not certain announcing the landlord's death to the whole pub was a good way of avoiding attention," she said ruefully. "Everyone knows our faces now."

"Perhaps we can make it work in our favour," John insisted. "We've got something in common with everyone here now. We can talk to them about poor old Seb, and they won't be so suspicious."

His instincts proved to be right. The regulars were much more willing to talk now that they had something in common to talk about. All Beth's money had gone, but John still had some silver that Strange had given them for expenses, so it was easy to keep the drinks coming in Peters' memory.

When John offered to buy a drink for a man with straggly ginger hair and a notch-shaped scar in his upper lip, Beth's ears pricked up at the name he gave: Robert Mott. Her eyes met John's and he nodded, recognizing the same thing. RM – the fourth set of initials on the paper. His table was right near the booth, and Beth watched and listened closely as he began to talk.

"They don't make 'em like Sebastian Peters any more,"

Mott declared drowsily, wiping the beer froth from his stubble with the back of his sleeve. "If you hadn't the money to eat, Seb would see you right 'til you could pay him back. A saint, that man was!"

Mott was blinking rapidly and his lips were trembling.

"You'll have another?" John was already sliding the money across.

"Aye." Mott seemed to come to his senses. "You're all right, son. Good lad." He drank deep and coughed. "Damn the plague. Rot its bloody bones. It's took away my trade and now it's took away the best man in London. A better man than that fool of a King…"

Beth's ears pricked up as she sat listening, and she saw John's eyes widen as a quick flash of fear shot through him. Did the man know something? Did he suspect then and was trying to trap them? *Stay calm, John*, Beth thought urgently.

Keeping his voice neutral, John asked, "What's your trade?"

"Bell founder," Mott said gloomily. "Bells ringing all over London, ringing for the dead, and the man who makes 'em can't make ends meet! I haven't had an order in weeks! Nobody dares set foot in the city with the plague abroad."

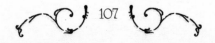

"It's the same all over," agreed John. "Money's scarce." Then, making it sound like an afterthought, he added, "Though there's plenty being spent on fancy palaces and jewelled coronets…"

Mott looked at him with red, impenetrable eyes. Then, in a low voice full of venom, the man burst out "You don't know the ruddy half of it!"

"Didn't mean no offence," John said hastily.

Mott sneered. "You've much to learn about the state of this nation, son. Where do you think the money for all them royal fripperies comes from? Out of the pockets of men like me!"

"Taxes," John said, with a disgusted shake of his head.

"They'd tax the bread from out your mouth, this government would!"

"Where I come from, they still talk about the Ship Tax," John said. Beth's heart was in her mouth, praying that her friend's gamble would pay off. Charles I had introduced the hated Ship Tax to pay for the cost of his Navy, and many people believed it was the spark that had ignited the Civil War. If Mott really were a Republican, this would flush him out.

But Mott didn't answer at all. He just drank down his whole tankard of beer in one draught and held it

out to John for another. Only when John brought a full tankard back did the man speak again.

"Restoration of the blasted monarchy," Mott said, spraying saliva as he did. "All so the King can sit on a velvet cushion eatin' quails while the poor honest working man has to go begging in the street! It's a wickedness, Jack. New taxes. New regulations. Can't trade outside of this district or that one without papers. Can't sell without the King skimming the cream off the top. Can't even wipe your nose without paying some fee to some bloodsucking leech."

He's deep in his cups now, Beth thought eagerly. *He can't even remember John's name. He's hooked him now. Time to reel him in.*

"My father used to say the same," John told Mott. "Promised us it would all be different when Parliament was in charge. He had such hope."

Mott just looked at him glassy-eyed. Either he was drunker than they had realized, or he was trying to work out if John was a liar.

"He taught us all the songs," John said, choking with feigned emotion. *"Babylon is fallen, is fallen, is fallen! Babylon has fallen, to rise no more…"*

It was the hymn Cromwell's New Model Army had

109

sung, celebrating the destruction of the monarchy and the death of the last King.

"Keep it down, you damn fool!" Mott snapped. "D'you want the whole street to hear you?" He leaned in and whispered low, "There's a proper time and place for such songs and this is neither."

"Babylon rose again, though, didn't it?" John scowled. "Perhaps honest men could tear it down again."

Mott was about to speak, then checked himself. "I've taken much strong drink," he decided. He stood, swaying, holding onto the back of the chair for support. "I'm for my bed."

"I'll see you home," John said quickly. "Where did you say your foundry was?"

"Whitechapel," Mott said. "But I'll walk alone. Don't need no *boy* to help me."

Crashing into several tables and knocking down a chair on his way to the door, Robert Mott stumbled out of the inn.

John rushed to Beth's side the second he was out of sight.

"The man's a conspirator, Beth. I'd bet my life on it! I found out where he works too."

"I think you're right. We have to search his house! But

where's Ralph? We'd better go and look for him…"

Beth headed out into the street and, to her relief, saw the cellar trap door was still open. She leaned down and peered into the gloom but there was no sign of Ralph. A moment later, she saw his pale face pop up from behind a barrel. "Psst!" he called. "Get down here, quick!"

"What is it?"

"Signs of conspiracy, or I'm a Turk!"

Ralph pulled a barrel over for them to use as a step, and the two quickly climbed down to join him in the cellar. Ralph pointed over to a far corner, where half-casks that once held beer had been pulled into a square. In the middle was another cask, where the melted stub of a candle stood.

"Chairs and a table," Beth breathed. "A secret meeting place."

"That's not all," Ralph said. "Look!"

On the wall behind, four familiar sets of initials had been scrawled darkly onto the brickwork:

S P
L B
J L
R M

"What are they written in?" John said, puzzled. "That's not paint, is it…?"

"Not likely," muttered Ralph.

A cold fist tightened around Beth's heart. "It's blood."

Chapter Ten
The Bell Foundry

A sign jutted out into the street above the door of a tall building. Three bells shone on it, gold against a deep blue background. From within came the sound of crackling flames, the ring of metal on metal, and the occasional screech of a grindstone. Beth felt that now-familiar sensation of excitement, fear and an odd clarity as she, John and Ralph crouched behind a low wall across the street, planning their next move. She knew she was well suited to the life of a spy – thoughts of weariness or hunger hadn't even crossed her mind.

The house in whose front yard they crouched was

shuttered up, its door branded with a red X. Nobody would be coming out to shoo them away, they knew that much.

"Finding the bell foundry wasn't hard," John mused. "Getting inside, well, that might be a little harder."

"By the sound of it, there's easily a half-dozen people still working in there," Ralph frowned. "How are we going to get our hands on Mott? Wait for them all to leave, then throw a bag over his head?"

"We can't confront Mott here," Beth said. "We need to find out where he lives. It's getting late. If we wait for them to close up shop, we can follow him home."

The sun had already begun to set over London, turning the street into an avenue of shadows. Only the distant flame of a street-corner fire gave any strong light. Some of the houses' windows still showed a weary glimmer as families began to gather for the evening meal, but many of them were as silent and dead as their former occupants.

Sure enough, it wasn't long before the first weary worker packed up and headed away from the bell foundry. Four more followed soon after, leather tradesmen's aprons folded over their arms, their hands blackened from long hours at the forge.

"Which one's Mott?" Ralph whispered.

"None of them!" Beth hissed, unable to hide her frustration as she peeked out from behind the brick wall, watching the men go past.

"He looked drunk out of his wits when he left the Four Swans," John said miserably. "Maybe he stopped to sleep it off in an alley somewhere."

"All the better for us if he has!" said Ralph. "We can break in and search his office. He's bound to have one in there…"

"Wait!" Beth said suddenly, pointing up. "There he is!"

Robert Mott's head and shoulders appeared at the very uppermost window of the foundry, a tiny casement just below the eaves. He yawned, smacked his lips, pulled the window shut, then retreated back inside.

"He's not wearing a shirt," Beth said. "It looks as though he's going to bed."

"Indeed," said Ralph. "Did you see the candle holder in his hand?"

"Of course!" John said. "His lodgings must be above the foundry. Mott doesn't have any other home than this!"

"All the other windows are dark," Beth noted. "There's

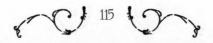

nobody but Mott to see us if we sneak inside, and he's retired to bed early…"

"Round the back, then," Ralph said determinedly. "Follow me."

A silent confidence settled on their friend, and he was in his element again, Beth knew. Stealthy entrances, back-alley adventures, midnight escapes – they were all meat and drink to Ralph. But she always had a feeling that his risk-taking attitude would get him into real danger one day…

A six-foot wall surrounded the foundry's back yard. A wooden door led through it, but it was bolted from within. Ralph studied the wall for a moment, deep in thought, then bounded forwards and grabbed the upper ledge with both hands. A second of scrambling, and he was up, straddling the wall like a boy on a horse.

"Nothing to it," he grinned. "Come on up, you two. There's nobody about."

"Be a gentleman and give me a lift up, would you?" Beth said to John, her eyes twinkling playfully. John, blushing furiously, laced his fingers together to make a step for her. Together he and Ralph hoisted her up and onto the wall. Scrabbling about like this wasn't exactly ladylike, she reflected with a wry smile, but spies couldn't afford to fret about such things when there was work to be done.

She dropped down neatly into the yard, her stage training affording her some skill in taking falls easily. She looked around her. The yard area was a mess, with broken pottery bell moulds lying around like the eggshells of monstrous birds. The smell of scorched metal was strong in the air; the foundry forges must still be warm from the day's work. A rickety-looking wooden staircase zigzagged up the back wall of the building, with doors at all three floors and a smaller door right at the top. That must lead into Mott's dwelling, the attic room.

John and Ralph jumped down behind her, John landing with a thump, Ralph light as a cat. Ralph tapped her on the shoulder and pointed up at a half-open window on the third floor.

"That's our way in," he said with a grin. "I love it when I don't even have to break anything."

"We're not going straight up to Mott's rooms?" John asked.

"Use your noddle, greenhorn," Ralph whispered, tapping his forehead. "Mott might be asleep, but he might not be. For all we know, he's waiting behind that door for us to burst in on him. We'll search the foundry

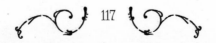

first, then call on Mott when it's good and dark and we're sure he's asleep."

"Agreed. Let's make a start." Beth began to climb, but winced as the staircase creaked alarmingly under her weight.

"On second thought, perhaps you two should wait until I'm inside before you climb up after me," she whispered back at them. "It'll be quieter. And safer!"

Don't look down, she told herself as she reached the second floor, but she couldn't help it. The jagged pot shards down in the yard looked like spikes ready to receive her falling body, and there was no railing on the side of the rickety staircase.

Trembling a little and breathing hard from the effort, she squeezed her way in through the window. It was still stifling hot inside the foundry. No wonder they'd left a window open despite the plague. In the gloom of the early evening she couldn't see much, but it was impossible to miss the huge iron bell hanging in the workshop's centre. A scaffold of wooden poles reaching from floor to ceiling held it off the ground. Workbenches stood against the walls, where half-finished bells lay among the clutter of tools.

Beth hesitantly approached the great bell, amazed

by its size. It was a wonder the floorboards didn't give way under the weight. It was taller than she was, and the clapper – fitted in place already, she saw – was almost as long as her own body.

"Look at that monster," Ralph whispered behind her, and she flinched at the sound of a voice. John was climbing in behind him, his face ashen from the climb. "Where do you think it's going to end up?"

"Some cathedral, surely," Beth replied.

"There's the foundry's mark," said Ralph quietly, pointing out the three bells on the inside surface. "It looks like this bell's almost finished."

"What's that up there, in the ceiling?" John was staring past the bell to the bare roof-beams and boards. "It looks like a trap door, but there's no stairs or ladder."

"That must be from an old grain lift," Ralph whispered. "The winch would have been up in the room above. Must be disused now. Nicely spotted, John. I reckon I can shinny up the scaffolding the bell's hanging from, open up that trap door and sneak right into Mott's attic!"

"So long as he hasn't put a table down on it, or a bed," John replied dubiously. "Why shouldn't he have, if the trap door's not in use any more? You'd make a right cake of yourself, hanging up there with no way in—"

"Why don't we search the workshop first," Beth cut in quickly, her voice low. "We're losing daylight, and it's not like we can spark up a lantern in here. We'd be seen."

Hurriedly they began to search. There was little to see but a medley of clay moulds, bricks, iron ingots and smithing tools. John found a drawer full of papers and brandished them excitedly, but they proved to be nothing more than the foundry accounts. All Ralph discovered was a cast-iron clapper used to make the inside of a bell ring. He tucked it into his waistband, insisting it could make a good missile.

Just as Beth was resigned to finding nothing, a tiny detail caught her eye. On the window ledge at the back of the room lay a thick layer of black soot, obviously not cleaned up for many a year. There were white marks in it where someone had been drawing with a fingertip.

She stared. One of the marks was a circle within a circle, with a line above it, just as in the note Tynesdale had found, and beside the circles was a clear capital letter B. The rest of the drawing had been smudged out – whether accidentally or deliberately, she couldn't tell.

"Look at this…" she hissed to the others.

They crowded round, glancing at one another as they

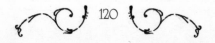

recognized the symbols.

"Look at the line," Beth said, pointing. "The way it curves – it looks almost like a map. That letter B could be telling us what the double circle means…"

"Barrel?" Ralph guessed. "Bell tower? Bomb?"

"It could be 'bell'," John said. "That looks like the beginning of an E next to the B."

Beth found a pencil and paper and quickly made a sketch of the markings. The double circle looked like a thick O, she thought in passing – and something suddenly flickered deep within her mind, like a silver fish flashing its scales before vanishing back into the lightless depths.

"Beth?" John asked.

Her brow was furrowed deep with sudden concentration. "Wait! I've got something … a line from Shakespeare…"

"Go on!"

"It's something I can remember, something so familiar I feel like I'll kick myself when I realize what it is…"

Ralph and John looked on, holding their breath.

Eventually Beth sighed and put the paper away. "It's no use. It's gone. For a moment there, I really thought … No, never mind."

"Well, we'd best get comfy," Ralph said in a hushed tone, sighing himself. "I reckon we need to give it an hour at least before we go calling on Mott."

"Who's for a game of noughts and crosses?" John said brightly.

Beth and Ralph looked at one another, and the scrappier boy rolled his eyes.

The darkness was almost absolute now. Only dim moonlight through the window gave enough light to see the vague shapes of objects around them. Beth strained her eyes to see the great bell, which hung in the room like a giant's helmet, its huge shadow the darkest place in the room.

Ralph stuck his head out of the rear window and looked up at Mott's attic. "No candlelight in the window," he reported back. "I reckon Mott's long since gone to sleep. It's time."

"Ralph, promise me you'll let John and me in through the door the moment you're up inside that attic," Beth insisted. "Even if Mott's asleep, he's still up there. And he's dangerous!"

"I'll go straight to the door and let you in," Ralph said. "Promise." He made a criss-cross sign over his heart and winked.

"Or I could climb up first…" John said bravely, but Ralph hushed him.

"Watch and learn, mate. This is how a seasoned spy does it."

Beth and John watched as Ralph scaled the scaffolding tower. He was up there quicker than a monkey, as if he were born to it. The bell stirred as his climbing shook the frame, swaying gently backwards and forwards, though thankfully not nearly enough to sound a peal. Beth's chest tightened as she watched him climb. Soon he was almost at the top, though the trapdoor wasn't directly above the scaffolding. Ralph would have to hold on with one arm and stretch out with the other to open it. If he fell, he'd surely break his neck.

Hold on, Ralph, Beth silently prayed.

"Easy does it," Ralph muttered to himself. He reached out and gently pushed the trap door upwards. It yielded without even a creak, and he looked down and gave Beth a grin of victory. He pushed it further up and over, careful not to let it fall with a crash, and when he was sure nothing was moving above his head, he gripped the lip of the opening with both hands, took a breath and swung out over the void.

But just as he did, a hairy, scarred hand shot down and grabbed Ralph's wrist.

"GOT YOU NOW, YOU LITTLE WEASEL!" roared a voice from above. It was Mott!

"Haul him up!" screeched another man's voice somewhere above them. "Don't drop him!"

"Drop him?" Mott boomed. "I'm going to *gut* him!"

Ralph fought to get out of Mott's grasp. With one flailing hand he regained his grip on the scaffolding pole and hung on.

Beth ran forward, thinking of nothing but the danger Ralph was in. She began to climb the scaffolding, reaching up for him, but he was still far too far away…

"It's a trap!" John yelled. "Ralph!"

Ralph was caught, painfully, between Mott and the scaffolding. He held onto the wood for dear life as Mott grunted and tugged at him, trying to pull him away and send him falling to his death. The other man was trying to grab Ralph too, his skinny pale arms lunging down from the trap door.

Ralph finally managed to break free from their grip, but he struggled to balance on the scaffolding, fumbled,

and fell. Beth stifled a scream as she saw him begin to plummet – but he was falling *inward*, towards the hanging bell, not out onto the floor far beneath!

Ralph flung his arms around the bell and clung to it, breaking his fall. It swung wildly, tolling its deep, mournful clang through the darkened building.

"Come on! We have to run!" John urged, pulling Beth's sleeve. "No sense in us all getting caught!"

Beth knew he was right – if she and John escaped, they might be able to rescue Ralph later. But if they were caught, they were all dead. Though her heart tightened at the thought of leaving their friend behind, they ran towards the open window and squeezed through it onto the rickety stairs as another deep deafening *bonggg* tolled behind them.

Beth looked back through the crack in the window desperately, but Ralph screamed at them to get out.

"Run! Save yourselves!"

Beth heard the door at the top of the stairs outside the building fly open. Heavy footsteps made the whole staircase wobble and shake, and without thinking, she jumped down the last three feet into the yard, staggering and gasping through the pot shards and nettles with John hot on her heels. She lurched for the bolt on the

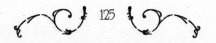

door that led out of the yard.

Strange, she had to reach Strange. He would know what to do…

The bell tolled again – just as thick, powerful arms grabbed her from behind. She struggled, but they were crushing her.

She couldn't move. She couldn't even breathe.

"You aren't going nowhere, sweetheart," Robert Mott's voice rasped in her ear.

Chapter Eleven
Kidnapped!

John, Beth and Ralph sat on the floor of Mott's attic, their backs against the bare brick wall, their legs sticking straight out in front of them. Their hands had been tied up behind their backs and Mott had been none too gentle doing it. Loops of cruelly tight, prickly hemp rope dug into Beth's wrists.

The attic was a cramped, narrow space, barely fit for habitation. The ceiling sloped diagonally down on both sides to meet the floor, with bare wooden props holding it up. The trap door, now closed, took up most of the room's centre portion. At one dingy end of the room was

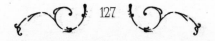

Mott's bed and the door; at the other, the empty space where the three of them now sat beneath a single grimy window.

"Who sent you?" Robert Mott demanded.

Behind him, his accomplice – the owner of the pale skinny arms that had grabbed at Ralph – clutched a pencil and paper, ready to write down the confessions that Mott was itching to beat out of them. The man looked pasty-faced and sick. Beth couldn't tell if it was the plague, the result of the same brutality Mott had shown to the three of them, or outright terror. Mott had called the man Leighton in a moment of anger, and Jack when he had calmed down: so, Jack Leighton. He must be JL from the paper. In spite of their predicament, Beth couldn't help feeling pleased – that only left LB unaccounted for on the mysterious list…

Not that finding another conspirator helps us right now if Mott wants to kill us, she thought. *And he'll make us talk first if he can.*

"I sneaked in on a dare!" Ralph was whining. "I don't know these two! Please, mister, you've got to let me go!"

"Liar," Mott sneered. "If you don't know 'em, why'd you shout for 'em to run and save themselves?"

"You *did* say you hadn't seen him before, Rob," Jack

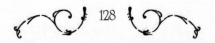

Leighton said cautiously, nodding towards Ralph. "He wasn't in the Four Swans with the other two, was he?"

Of course – Ralph had been exploring the cellar while John and Beth were upstairs. Mott hadn't seen his face. It was a threadbare gambit, but Beth prayed it might pay off. Especially if Leighton was as reluctant to shed blood as he seemed.

"Who cares if he weren't?" Mott yelled, rounding on his accomplice. "What's one less brat on the streets of London anyway?"

"W-we can't kill him if he's innocent," Leighton insisted.

"You can't have a revolution without spilling a bit of innocent blood!" Mott snarled. "And look at the company he keeps. Look at *this* lying little wretch." He pulled John's hair back hard, and Beth flinched.

"Robert, for pity's sake, they're just youngsters—!"

"Make yourself useful, you bloody fool, and go and fetch my carving knife," Mott snarled. "I'll soon have this one telling all he knows."

Beth glanced anxiously over at John, and she could see he was trying not to give any sign of how terrified he must be. She longed to reach over and reassure him, but there was nothing to be done.

129

"Who sent you?" Mott repeated angrily.

Nobody spoke.

He pulled a chair up in front of them and sat down on it while Leighton began to rummage through some drawers. "Come on, now. I *know* you're spies," he said, suddenly sounding almost reasonable. "And you're all as good as dead. Not a one of you is leaving this place alive. We'll kill you one by one, make the others watch, then burn your bodies in the forge downstairs—"

"You're bluffing!" John threw back in Mott's face. "You need us alive. Kill us, and you'll never know what we know!"

"I don't need *all* of yer!" Mott exploded with fury. "Maybe I'll save you for last, how about that? I'll do the young lady first, shall I? And you can watch me. How's that sound, Sir Galahad? Want to watch your pretty little friend cut to bits in front of you?"

Leighton silently passed Mott a long kitchen knife. Mott tested the edge on his thumb and nodded, satisfied.

"Don't touch her!" Ralph burst out. "Don't you lay a finger on her!"

"So, you *are* with them," Mott said, his lip curling viciously. "I knew it. Lie to me again, boy, and I'll slit your throat."

"We're not really going to kill 'em, are we?" Jack Leighton, said in a low voice from behind Mott, wringing his hands anxiously.

"Why not?" Robert demanded. "They deserve it. This one especially!" He stood up, strode over to John and spat full in his face. "You should have heard him, spinning his lies about his dear old dad teaching him the songs of Cromwell's army! I bet you think you made a proper fool out of me, don't you, boy?"

"Not any more," John said carefully. The spittle lay white and glistening on his cheek. "It looks like you've got the upper hand now, sir."

"So talk."

John grinned. "Why don't you fetch me a beer first? It's your turn to buy."

"Why, you little—" Mott swung his leg back and kicked John hard in the ribs, knocking the wind out of him and forcing tears into his eyes. Without pausing, he kicked again, this time in his thigh. He grabbed John's shirtfront and bashed his head against the brick wall behind.

"Think this is a game, do you?" he shouted. "Think this is funny, do you? You know what you are? You're a maggot!" He finally let John go and turned his back on them. John was left panting and slumped on the floorboards, doubled over with pain.

Beth struggled against her bonds, wishing again that she could lay a comforting hand on her friend. "Beating up a tied-up boy?" she demanded, glaring at Mott. "You're a filthy coward."

"*He's* the coward, not me! A spineless maggot, without the guts to be a King-killer!" Mott leered. "Oh, he knows the truth of things well enough. The King's sucking up all the wealth of this country to line his own pockets. He's nothing but a parasite. A bloated tick. Everyone knows it. But you brats just want to serve him, like a pack of grovelling mongrels!"

"He's our rightful King," John groaned. "Nothing … you can do … will change that."

"He'll be dead before the week's out!" Mott laughed, a harsh sound like the bark of a dog.

"Liar. There's no true plot," John spat blood onto the floor. "Just a drunkard's dreams."

He's goading him, Beth realized. *He's trying to draw him out. Oh, John, stop being so brave! He'll beat you to death, he means it!*

"You don't know nothing!" Mott raged. He turned and leaned back down, pressing the knife blade up to

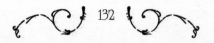

132

John's throat and held it there. "The plot's bigger than you could ever guess!"

"Is that right? Well, why don't you tell us your precious plot, then – prove it!" John coughed. "You're going to kill us anyway, aren't you? Or was that just another lie?"

For a moment, Mott really seemed like he might. He wanted to boast, and it was hurting him not to. But, in the end, his anger got the better of him and he lashed out with kicks again. His heavy boots smacked Ralph in the ribs, and then, relentless, he turned and kicked Beth hard in the shin. The pain burned, but she refused to cry or even utter a sound.

"Leave her alone!" Ralph shouted.

"Robert, for God's sake!" exploded Jack Leighton. "She's just a girl!"

"She's a little vixen, is what she is," raged Mott. "Don't waste your pity on her."

Leighton doesn't have the stomach for this, Beth realized hopefully through her pain. *He might be the weak link in the chain. Perhaps we can use that…*

"It's not right, I won't stand for it—"

"You'll damn well do as you're bid!" Mott roared at him. "Remember your oath! And as for this guttersnipe, she'll do as she's bid an' all!"

133

Wheeling around, he grabbed a clump of Beth's hair, wound it round his fist for a better grip, and pulled so hard that it ripped out of her scalp. Blinding red agony tore through her and her whole body trembled, not just from the pain but from the effort of holding it in.

I won't scream. I won't cry. I won't give him the satisfaction! She clenched her teeth so hard her jaw ached. Her eyes were brimming with tears, but she squeezed them shut and forced herself to think past the raging fire of pain. She took several deep breaths and eventually the pain began to pass.

"We have to talk about this!" Leighton was saying to Mott. "We're out of our depth here. Maybe we should bring in one of the others?"

"Don't gab in front of the prisoners, fool!" Mott grunted. "Come over here."

Mott and Leighton went and huddled in the far corner, talking in low voices. Beth's head was pounding, but she knew this was an important chance to get information, one she couldn't ignore. She made herself concentrate on the details of the room. She had to remember everything – any part of it might be significant later.

One bed, unmade, a simple pallet. A small chest of drawers beside the bed. A washstand. On top of it, a

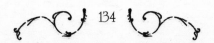

basin, a rusty razor and a shaving mirror, both thick with dust from long neglect. A fraying rug on the floor that just made the bare floorboards look all the more barren. Three shabby-looking chairs, the one Mott had sat on in front of them, the other two by the fire. A small three-legged pot for the coal. A stand of fire tools.

And a mantelpiece above the fire.

Sitting on it, a three-armed candlestick that was the only source of light, a bone comb, a pair of pliers probably borrowed from the foundry downstairs, and an old pewter mug bent out of shape. The clutter of a bachelor who cared little about himself or anyone else – nothing out of the ordinary, it seemed. But propped on the end of the mantelpiece was a pencil sketch on a sheet of paper. Beth saw instantly that the paper was white, though the mantelpiece would see plenty of sunlight through the window. If it were old, dust and sun would have yellowed it, so she knew it hadn't been there for long.

She strained to see the sketch properly in the dancing light of the candles. It was some sort of map, with buildings and open areas marked out, and one wide stripe of wavy lines in the midst. Sudden excitement struck her as she recognized it. This was the same image she'd seen drawn in the dust of the window ledge! That had been a crude version of a map.

Yes – there was a building that looked like two circles, one within the other. It was very close to the wavy lines. Those must represent a river – the Thames, perhaps, or … Did the conspirators know the King was in Oxford? It could be the Isis, the part of the Thames that flowed through there. Her heart raced at the thought.

Mott glanced back at her, his face twisted in brutal anger, and Beth quickly looked away, hoping the shadows of the candlelight had hidden where she had been gazing. If Mott knew what she'd been up to, he'd kill her for sure.

But if he had noticed, he didn't give any sign. Instead, he seemed to be getting angrier and angrier with Leighton.

"You know we can't let them go!" he yelled. "They'd go straight to the law!"

"B-but it's cold-blooded murder!" whined Leighton.

"Should have thought of that before you helped me catch 'em!" Mott bellowed in his face. "Why'd you sign up with us if you don't have the stomach for killing, eh? Eh?"

"I signed up to kill a tyrant, not a helpless girl!"

Leighton retorted.

"Your fine sentiments will see us all strung up at Tyburn!" Mott screeched. "Damn your eyes, man, I'll slaughter 'em all myself and have done!" Carving knife in hand, he came storming back towards the three of them.

Beth's eyes widened with panic.

"Time to start spillin' guts," Mott snarled. "Don't struggle and it'll be over all the quicker…"

Chapter Twelve

Tables Turned

Mott grabbed John's shoulder with his left hand to keep him still and drew back the knife with his right. Beth knew exactly what he was going to do. Mott would shove the blade up under John's ribcage and into his heart. She let out a cry in spite of herself.

But to her shock, as Mott went to drive the knife home, Ralph brought his foot up in a vicious kick. His boot slammed into Mott's arm with a heavy thump. His hands were tied, but Mott hadn't bothered to tie his legs, and the kick took the evil man completely by surprise. The knife, knocked out of his grip, went flying across the room, then fell spinning to the floor, skidded and finally vanished under the bed.

Mott let go of John and grabbed Ralph by his shirtfront. A nasty grimace spread over his face as he hauled Ralph to his feet.

"Grab that blasted knife, Leighton!" he yelled to the other man. "As for you, boy, no quick and clean death for you. I'll dash your brains out!"

To prove he meant it, he whacked Ralph's head against the wall behind and Beth stared in anguish as she saw her friend go limp. But as Mott prepared to smash him into the wall a second time to finish the job, Ralph quickly head-butted Mott right on the bridge of the nose – he'd been faking! There was a gruesome *crack* and Mott fell backwards, howling, clutching his eyes. Blood poured down his face.

"I'm blind!" he roared through his bloodstained fingers. "Filthy, dirty-fighting little rat blinded me! Leighton, kill them!"

Leighton was still rummaging around under the bed, trying to grab for the knife.

Quickly, while both of the conspirators were out of action, Beth saw Ralph wrench hard at his bonds. He soon managed to pull one hand free, though it was

rubbed raw and sore. He swiftly undid the other hand, just as Leighton stood up triumphantly, clutching the knife. "I've got it!"

"Then kill them, damn you!" Mott yelled again. He shook his head, sending droplets of blood flying, and rubbed at his eyes trying to clear the gore out of them.

Hesitantly, Leighton edged across the room, wielding the knife as if he didn't know which end to hold it by.

"Ralph!" Beth shouted, then held her breath as Ralph made a split-second decision. He could untie them, or try to fight Leighton off. But if Leighton worked up the courage to stab him while he was untying John or Beth, he'd be defenceless.

Ralph made his choice: he took a deep breath and pulled John to his feet as he was closest. He tugged frantically at the heavy knots, trying to free John's hands as quickly as he could before Leighton managed to attack.

"What are you waiting for?" Mott screeched. "Useless fool, I'll feed you to the crows!"

Ralph gave one last tug, and John's hands were free.

"Thanks!" John gasped, rubbing his wrists. "I'm in your debt."

"No, you're not," Ralph panted quickly. "We watch

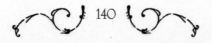

out for one another. That's the code."

Leighton lurched towards them, but he looked more uncertain than ever now that he was facing off against two of them. He jabbed at Ralph, a half-hearted effort that the boy dodged easily.

"Over there!" Beth cried, nodding towards the washstand. Ralph quickly snatched up the rusty shaving razor. Now he had a blade too. John's eyes darted uncertainly between Beth and Ralph, unsure who to help first.

"Come a little closer," Ralph was saying to Leighton, with a slow smile. "Let's have it out. Blade to blade. You and me…"

Leighton's eyes widened and he actually took a step back. His boot heels rang hollow on the trap door as he passed over it.

"Give me that damned knife, you dolt," Mott exploded, out of his mind with rage, still squinting through bloodied eyes. He grabbed the blade out of Leighton's hand. "If you want something done properly, you have to do it yourself!"

Leighton shrank to the back of the room, mumbling and shaking his head in fear.

Just then, seemingly struck by a sudden idea, John

lunged forward and pulled the trap door open. Now there was a lethal drop between Mott and them. He'd have to edge round the side if he wanted to attack.

"John! The poker!" Beth yelled from the floor. "Grab it!"

John looked baffled for a moment, then the meaning of Beth's words hit home. Mott was already attempting to skirt round the trap door towards him, and John darted towards the fireplace and snatched up the poker, holding it out in front of him.

While there was a distraction, Ralph took the opportunity to dash to Beth's side, and the razor quickly sawed through the ropes binding her hands. She let out a sigh of relief, though not taking her eyes of the approaching figure of Mott. He was now edging past the fireplace. The space between the chimney breast and the open trap door was only two feet wide, and he and John faced off in the middle of it. It was like watching duellists fighting on a broad plank.

"That one can fight," Mott sneered, nodding at Ralph. His bristly chin was crusted with blood. "He's street-bred. But I'll wager you can't, little Sir Galahad."

"Try me," John said through clenched teeth, wielding the poker.

Behind Mott, the door slammed shut. Leighton had fled, his nerve finally broken completely. Beth heard the sound of his retreating footfalls on the rickety stairs outside.

"Damn you for a coward, Jack Leighton!" Mott bellowed back at him. "When the great day comes, you'll be torn to bits like that parasite of a King! You'll be—"

While Mott was distracted, John seized the moment. He slammed the poker into Mott's stomach, cutting his words short, and the man's eyes bulged white in his crimson face. His cheeks puffed out and he sank to his knees.

John bashed him again, this time on the shoulder, hard. Something cracked, and the knife fell from Mott's hand through the open trap door, clattering on the distant floor far below.

Mott teetered on the edge of the void, about to fall in after it.

Ralph shouted in glee, "Give him another one like that, John! Knock him down the hole!"

But John pulled the trap door shut, letting Mott collapse writhing onto the boards. Beth exhaled. "Let's tie him up," John said, breathing hard. "We need him alive."

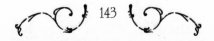

"I bloody don't!" Ralph sneered.

"Tie him up!" Beth asserted. She threw the loose ropes across to John. "You can argue about it later!"

Ralph angrily folded away the razor and set to work with the ropes.

"Should we get after Leighton?" John asked. "He might be fetching help!"

Beth shook her head. "There's no point. He'll be a good distance away by now. He seemed well out of it."

Mott groaned as Ralph looped the rope around his hands. "Get me to a doctor! I-I think my arm's broke!"

"I think not," said Beth coldly.

"You ditch-born dirty-fighting little scabs—"

Ralph gave him a kick in the ribs for good measure. "Hold still and shut your face, or I'll give you something to moan about," he warned.

Together, they bound Mott's hands and feet, leaving him trussed like a turkey on the floor. He swore and yelled until Ralph shoved a rag into his mouth and tied a kerchief around it to keep it in place. After that he made struggling pained sounds, but couldn't speak another word.

"Well, he's not going anywhere now," John said when they were done. He mopped the sweat of exertion from

 144

his face with his sleeve. "What should we do now? Send for Strange?"

"Shh," Beth admonished quickly, nodding towards their prisoner. But Ralph remained quiet, staring seethingly at Mott.

"Ralph?" Beth said, looking at him curiously.

"I don't see why he deserves any mercy," Ralph said scornfully.

"We have a code—" Beth began, but Ralph cut her off.

"I reckon certain people don't deserve to be held to no code." He clenched his teeth and Beth and John both frowned at him.

"What are you talking about?" John said, taking a step forward.

"This old razor hasn't got much of an edge on it, but it'll do the job…" Ralph said coldly.

Beth and John stared at him in horror. Beth suddenly felt like the young man she knew had gone. This pale, blood-spattered boy with murder in his eyes was a stranger to her.

Ralph looked at their dumbstruck faces. "You can't be thinking o' letting him get away with it!" he said furiously. "Didn't you hear what this sack of guts said?"

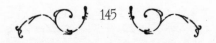

"Ralph, calm down!" Beth pleaded.

"He was ready to kill us! If I hadn't have kicked him when I did, we'd all be cold corpses now!"

"He's our prisoner!"

"You know what the Bible says, Beth. An eye for an eye, a life for a life. Prisoner or not, he dies—"

"We can't kill him!" John burst out.

"Stand back and watch, then, if you're too dainty to get your hands bloody! You two don't have the stomach for the real nitty-gritty of our line of work? Very well, I'll do it myself!"

Beth's blood ran cold as she realized she'd heard those very words before, only minutes ago. *Are we no better than the King-killers?*

But Ralph was already brandishing the razor.

Chapter Thirteen

Justice?

Beth laid a hand on Ralph's shoulder. "Please, Ralph, think! What does the spy code say about killing?"

Ralph shrugged her hand off, but muttered, "'A spy kills only when his own life is in danger, or to save an innocent victim.' There. Chapter and verse, from the Strange manual of spycraft."

"I see no innocent victims that require saving, do you?"

"No," Ralph admitted grudgingly.

"Well, then – is your life in danger?"

"Of course it is! He tried to kill us!" Ralph insisted.

"*Tried*," John put in. "And he failed."

Beth nodded. "We were in danger then, but we're not now. Look at him – he's helpless. He's no threat to anyone."

"Don't tell me he doesn't deserve to die!" Ralph was growing desperate now. "He's plotting to kill the King, for God's sake!"

"And Strange will see he faces justice for it," Beth told him more firmly.

"Why wait for Strange? Let's make our own justice! Mott's just as dead whether he dies here or on the gallows, ain't he?"

Beth grabbed Ralph's arm. "Cutting his throat with a razor while he's tied up is not justice, Ralph. It's revenge. Don't pretend you don't know that."

His tensed arm felt like an iron bar in her fingers. He gave Mott a ferocious, hungry look, like a wolf that craves to sink its fangs into human flesh. But then finally he gave a long, deep sigh and Beth felt his muscles relax.

"Ah, he ain't worth it." Ralph flung the razor to the back of the room.

Beth felt her body sag with relief. *That's the Ralph I know*, she thought. *Thank heavens.* She suddenly felt drained and exhausted with all that had happened that night.

"Good man," John said proudly, giving Ralph a pat on the back. "I knew you had it in you—"

Beth saw Ralph flinch, and wished John hadn't said that. They were all still on edge.

"Why don't you run and fetch Strange?" she quickly told John. "Ralph and I can guard Mott while you're gone." *And Ralph will calm down all the quicker if you're not patronizing him*, she thought.

"Er, excellent plan, Beth," John said, catching her eye. "I'll be back as quick as I can!"

"Watch out for Leighton," Ralph snapped as John headed out through the door. "He's still out there, remember!"

Ten minutes passed, then thirty, then a whole hour. Every minute that John was gone was an agony to Beth. She'd gone for almost an entire day without sleep, and Ralph's final warning to John conjured dreadful images in her mind.

"He *is* coming back, Beth," Ralph said quietly. "You've got to have some faith."

Beth didn't reply. What if John never came back? Leighton could have been waiting for him round the very first corner. She and Ralph might sit here for hours waiting for Strange to respond to a message that had never been delivered. What if Leighton's backup arrived before theirs? Just thinking about the possibility of John not returning made her stomach lurch – and, she had to admit – her heart twist.

She went from window to door and back to window, watching, alert for the slightest sound of a footfall on the back stairs or the front door opening. Despite all Ralph's urging, she couldn't sit and rest, although she knew she should. Once, she glanced into Robert Mott's hate-filled eyes, and his gloating pleasure at her worries made her turn away again quickly.

Finally a clatter of hooves came from outside as a coach drew up, and Beth snapped to attention. Moments later, she heard footsteps and hushed voices. People were coming up the back staircase. But was it John?

All her fears vanished as her friend burst into the room, followed by two cloaked men she didn't recognize. John was gasping for breath, as if he'd run halfway around London and back.

"This is the conspirator?" one of the cloaked men

said, jabbing his thumb towards Mott.

"Yes," Beth said. Carefully, taking her time, she explained everything they had learned. The men listened as silently as ravens, and with as little show of emotion. They must be two of Strange's "cloak-and-dagger men", as Ralph called them – senior spies who specialized in whisking enemies of the Crown away to secret prisons…

When Beth had finished, the men pulled Mott to his feet. "We'll take him into custody," the one who had spoken said gruffly. "Don't concern yourselves with him any more. He's ours now."

"Do you think he'll talk?" John asked, with a doubtful frown.

The spy snorted. "Strange will have him singing like a nightingale. He has his funny little ways."

"I don't know. Mott seemed pretty tough—"

"They all break sooner or later, son," the man retorted swiftly. "Sometimes the tough ones are the most brittle."

Beth wasn't sorry to see them leave. The men had a cold-blooded way about them that chilled her. From the window she watched them bundling Mott into the carriage, and thought of spiders carrying a swaddled fly.

Then the coach was gone, as if it had never been there.

"Sun's coming up," Ralph said, stretching and

yawning. "Where to now?"

"Back to the safe house in Threadneedle Street," Beth said firmly. "We need to go over everything we've learned. Every clue, every scrap of information we remember."

"Agreed," said John. "We still need to work out what exactly the plot against the King is. We can't lose momentum."

"Mott knows," Ralph reminded them. "Those spies thought Strange would get him to talk…"

But Beth was already on her way out of the door. "What if he can't? If Mott clams up, holds out for long enough, or if he dies, then we're the only ones who have a chance of preventing whatever is about to happen!" She paused and turned back quickly to grab the crude map she'd seen on the mantelpiece. "We might need this. Now – let's go."

As the trio made their way wearily back through the London streets, Beth saw the light of morning dawn on the night's fresh crop of human misery. The bodies of those who had died in the night lay sprawled in the gutters, and several times they had to cross the street to avoid stepping on the dead.

At least the they suffer no more, she thought to herself. *It's the living who deserve our pity.*

Up ahead, a man was hammering on the door of a house. His face and neck were covered with the disfiguring lumps and boils of the plague.

"Let me in, Lottie!" he begged. "It's me! It's your Bill!"

"Go away!" shrieked a voice from the upstairs window. "We shan't let you in – we can't!"

"Let me see the children," Bill howled. "They need their daddy – who's going to kiss them goodnight if not me?"

The woman in the house gave a terrible forlorn cry, as if her heart were breaking in her chest. Then the solemn face of a small boy appeared at the window.

"Mummy says you can't come in," the boy said. "You'll bring plague into the house."

"Tim?" Bill pleaded, with a pathetic fresh hope in his voice. "Good boy! Come down the stairs and open the door!"

The boy slowly closed the window shutters.

Beth had a lump in her throat as she passed by the doomed man locked out of his own house. His cries echoed in her ears long after she had left the street.

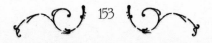

And yet the city was waking up around them. Those citizens who had survived the night were emerging, weary and red-eyed, into the morning light. Traders began to get on with the business of the day, setting out stalls, opening shop shutters and taking up familiar places on street corners, because life had to go on for those who were still there to live it. A cart laden with cabbages passed by, sending up clouds of dust, and Ralph coughed as the dust caught in his throat. Before Beth could even protest, a flower-seller had grabbed her arm and pulled her away.

"It's for your own good, miss!" the flower-seller insisted. "He's got the plague!"

"He hasn't!" Beth said indignantly, fighting to get away.

"You'll thank me for it later, when you're not dead," the woman barked. With a painful wrench, Beth tugged herself free and ran back to join her friends.

"You'll be sorry!" the flower-seller yelled after her.

Beth couldn't wait to get inside the safe house, despite it not being her familiar home at the Peacock and Pie, with the jolly welcome from Big Moll and the eager face of her dear friend Maisie. Though she loved her adventures as a spy, at that moment she missed them

so much it hurt. But at least young Maisie was safe in Oxford with the rest of the company…

Just as they were about to reach the house, Beth spotted a familiar face on the other side of the road – it was Clare Smythe, one of the theatre's loyal staff who kept the costumes laundered and mended.

"Clare!" she called, dashing across the street. "Oh, Clare, it's wonderful to see you! You're well? And who's this?" She bent down to the tearful child whose hand Clare was holding. "Can this really be little Maddy, who I used to rock in my arms? Look how big you are!"

"Hello, Beth!" Clare exclaimed, and kissed her on both cheeks, then frowned. "My darling girl, but whatever are you doing here? Aren't you meant to be off in Oxford with the rest of the troupe?"

"Uh … an old friend is very ill," Beth explained, then changed the subject quickly. "But come now, what's the matter with little Maddy? A face as pretty as yours shouldn't be all filled with tears."

"I wanted to see the lion," Maddy said, pressing a knuckle into her watering eye. "He was in a big cage and the cage was on a big cart and I wanted to see him and they wouldn't let me…!"

"A lion?" Beth repeated, amazed at what the child

had said.

"She's telling the truth, bless her," said Clare. "Down in Southwark, I swear to God, there was a cage with a lion in it! It must have come from the Tower – you know, where the menagerie is."

"Goodness! What was it doing outside the grounds?" laughed Beth. This had been a long, nightmarish night, and now it seemed to be turning into a morning straight out of a pantomime.

"Well, I shouldn't like to say," Clare said, leaning in close. "Not in front of Maddy, I mean. But it was just by the Hope Theatre, and you know what goes on there, I trust…"

"Oh." Beth tried not to let her dismay show, or little Maddy might start crying again.

She knew all too well what Clare was driving at. The Hope Theatre wasn't just used for plays. It sometimes played host to a nastier spectacle – animal-baiting. Mostly it was bears who were tormented for the audience's entertainment, but other animals had met that fate too, including – though very rarely – lions. *This must be someone's idea of a special occasion*, Beth thought, feeling a little sick.

"Well, we must hurry on," she said. "God bless, Clare.

 156

Goodbye, Maddy dear. I'll see you both soon!"

"God bless. I hope to see you on the stage again soon, Miss Beth," Clare said.

Beth's shoulders sagged as they hurried on – Clare's words had reminded her of Lady Lucy back in Oxford. There was no way she'd be back in time to play her starring role, not with the plot against the King still ripe, its secrets not yet uncovered. No doubt Lady Lucy Joseph was revelling in taking Beth's lead part right at that very moment.

Finally they reached the safe house, and once inside with the door locked and bolted, Beth, John and Ralph gathered around the table. Beth smoothed out the vital piece of paper in front of them, along with the map she'd pocketed from Robert Mott's attic mantelpiece.

"We believe we know now who three of the four conspirators are now," Beth began. "SP was Sebastian Peters. RM is Robert Mott. JL is Jack Leighton, still at large. The only one who's still a mystery is LB."

"I looked through the foundry accounts in case any of the workers was an LB," said John. "None of them was."

"Didn't find an LB at the Four Swans, neither," said Ralph.

"We know what the plotters want," Beth went on.

"They're going to make an attempt on the King's life. But we don't know where or when, or even how."

"The details must be in the drawing," John said. "If the note is an instruction of some sort from Vale, that could be how he was confirming the plot. There must be something in it we've missed…"

"Wavy lines mean water, Sandford said." Beth pointed at them. "And the bridge may denote a First Son, but it might also genuinely mean a bridge – and a bridge on water means a river. I think it simply means the Thames."

"Just a moment – show us that map you got from Mott's place again," Ralph said. Excitement was creeping into his voice, and as Beth unfolded it, he stabbed his finger on a double dotted line that led across the central river. "That's the Thames, all right! There's London Bridge, and there's the Isle of Dogs … so that circle thing near the South Bank might be the Beargarden."

Beth froze. Gooseflesh rose on her arms. Everything fell into place in one terrifying instant.

"The Beargarden," she breathed. "It was right in front of us at the foundry!"

"Eh?" John said, looking between the others with confusion on his face.

"That drawing in the dust on the window ledge –

the two circles, and the B with the beginning of an E! Someone wrote Beargarden, then rubbed it out!"

John frowned. "But the Beargarden isn't its real name, is it? That's just the nickname for—"

"—the Hope Theatre," Beth finished. *Where they bait live animals as entertainment, as Clare had just mentioned.* The line from Shakespeare she'd struggled to remember at the bell foundry fell into her mind now. In *Henry V*, Shakespeare had referred to the Globe Theatre as a "wooden O", because of its circular shape. Just like the Hope Theatre – or the Beargarden as London folk call it!

"But all the theatres are shut because of the plague, as you know," Ralph pointed out.

"Unless this is about some special, private performance?" suggested John.

Beth pointed at the lion's head on the paper. "I know exactly what the special performance is. They're going to bait a lion to death. And God help us all, I think I know why…"

Chapter Fourteen

A Strange Meeting

At the top of the bell tower at St Paul's Cathedral, Strange listened in silence as Beth explained what they had discovered, as John and Ralph watched and listened grimly, interjecting when necessary. For all the emotion he showed, his craggy, impassive face could have been a stone gargoyle's. When Beth mentioned Sebastian Peters, he held up a hand for her to stop. "This man, Peters. Did you happen to discover his nationality?"

"We never spoke to him. He died before we reached him."

"Nobody else mentioned it?"

Beth searched her memory, and looked to John who shook his head. "No."

Strange nodded. "Continue."

He remained stock still until Beth mentioned the Beargarden. Suddenly, Strange's face came alive. He was on his feet and by her side in two quick strides.

"You're certain that's what the message meant?"

"I'm certain," Beth said. "It all fits together. The water, the circles, the lion's head. There's only one part that's still missing."

"And that is?" Strange snapped.

"How the King would be in attendance at a session of lion-baiting at the Beargarden in London," Beth said slowly, "when His Majesty is currently in Oxford along with the rest of his court…"

Strange frowned at her, and Beth's heart quickened involuntarily.

"I see. Pray tell, Miss Johnson, why you are so certain that the lion-baiting is for the King's benefit?"

"Because it is traditional, when an ambassador visits on state business, to offer them the entertainment they most wish to see," Beth explained, managing to keep her speech calm. "His Majesty is keen to build a secret diplomatic alliance with Germany, is he not?"

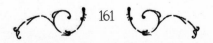

"Go on," Strange said.

"Blood sports are even more popular with the German nobles than they are with the English," Beth continued, careful to keep the distaste out of her voice. "If the King is secretly meeting with a German ambassador, with a view to making an alliance, then he will want to offer him a special kind of entertainment. Something rare and to his taste … such as baiting a lion in the Beargarden."

Strange fixed her with his gaze, and then – to her astonishment – he smiled slowly. It was not a regular phenomenon. She glanced at Ralph, who raised an eyebrow too.

"You are good, Beth," he said. "I set you to work finding out the enemy's secrets, but you appear to have uncovered some of our own…"

"The King's not in Oxford at all, is he?" Beth said, certain now.

"No," Strange confessed. "In truth, His Majesty never left. He is residing in London in secret, preparing to meet with the German ambassador."

Beth thought of the company back in Oxford, and felt a sly satisfaction that Lady Lucy Joseph wouldn't be performing for her cousin the King at all, even if she had stolen Beth's part. Not that she had seemed all that interested in a royal audience…

"But what of the plague?" John said, frowning. "Is it not still too dangerous?"

"The ambassador insisted, and the King and his court have been careful not to allow anyone even slightly associated with those afflicted with the disease to come close. Beth, your analysis of the situation was correct in every detail," Strange continued. "Ambassador Von Karstein of Germany likes nothing better than to watch a captive animal fighting off a pack of trained hounds. His Majesty was advised that baiting a lion would be a suitably rare spectacle to impress the ambassador."

Mors ad Regi, Beth thought. *Death to the King.* The lion was the king of beasts. It sickened her to think of such a noble creature condemned to a painful death in the name of entertainment – even if it was for the sake of England, she couldn't help thinking it was wrong.

Strange continued, "I admit, I am impressed with your work – but also gravely concerned. His Majesty's meeting at the Beargarden was supposed to be a state secret. Yet, somehow, the conspirators must know that the King is in London. They know about the meeting." Strange slammed his fist down on the ledge. "Someone right within the King's inner circle is passing on information."

"Perhaps it is the fourth conspirator," Beth suggested. "Is there a L.B. in the King's court?"

Strange stood still with his knuckles pressed to his forehead. The master spy's brain was like a library, meticulously ordered, with nothing out of place. Beth knew he was hunting through names, looking for a match as if he were leafing through a book.

"There is no LB," he said finally.

"You always tell us not to make assumptions," John said tentatively. "What if we've assumed something about LB?"

"Such as?"

"What if one of the letters isn't a name? What if it's a title? Lord Beaumont, Lady Belvedere, something of that kind?"

Beth felt a chill. "Lord Beaumont is head of the College of Arms, where the heralds work." Including my friend, Francis Sandford, she thought. "And there was heraldry in the symbols on that note."

"The heraldry is what convinces me Henry Vale is behind this," Strange said. "The bridge must be his symbol for himself, the mark of the First Son."

"Vale's made his last mistake, then. We can catch

him when he attacks the King!" Ralph said excitedly. "Execute him properly this time!"

"Vale will not attack in person. His agents will attempt the assassination in his name." Strange sighed. "I doubt Vale is even in the country. The danger of discovery is far too great. I believe he is working abroad; we have intelligence that he's in Germany recruiting foreign agents to his cause."

Beth had a horrible thought. "An attempt on the King's life during a diplomatic meeting could plunge the whole country into a new war!"

"Indeed." Strange's voice was stony.

"What if – God forbid – His Majesty were killed, and Germany were blamed for it?"

"I suspect that may be exactly what the conspirators hope to achieve," Strange said. "We know this much, at least, thanks to you: the conspirators plan to strike while the lion-baiting takes place. We can be ready for them."

"What? You're not going to allow the lion-baiting to go ahead!" exclaimed John, aghast. "I apologize, sir, but we've found out about the plot, so surely you have to cancel the meeting?"

"I cannot," Strange said.

"But surely you must? The King is in danger—"

"Boy, the danger would be all the worse if the King withdrew!" Strange retorted, silencing John. "The conspirators would know immediately that we had uncovered their plot. They would melt back into the shadows and bide their time until the *next* plot – and we might not be lucky enough to uncover that one."

John's cheeks were red. "So we're just going to let them try to kill the King?" he said.

"We will watch from the shadows and catch them in the act," said Strange, with a firm reassuring hand on John's shoulder. "We do not have much time. The meeting begins in an hour."

"We're going to help your men protect the King?" Beth felt thrilled to be working alongside the master spy himself. Strange had never put such trust in her before.

"No. When I said *we* would be ready for them, I meant *solely* the four of us." He drew a dusty sack from the corner of the room. "My best men are dead from the plague. Others are too far away to help. We four are all that stands between the Crown and anarchy."

High on the bell tower, Beth felt momentarily dazed. Strange's matter-of-fact words had left her reeling – they were being entrusted with something very important indeed, once again: the life of the King.

"But … what about the King's guards?" she managed to ask. "Can't you just surround him with them?"

"Everything you have uncovered points to a traitor within the King's own household," Strange said through clenched teeth. "If I double the King's guard, the traitor will know his plans are found out. We must act so as to convince him we are none the wiser."

Beth swallowed hard and nodded. "Understood, sir."

"Good. Besides, I do not imagine either the King's guard or the conspirators know their way around a theatre nearly as well as you do." Strange rewarded her with another rare smile. "Our blessings are precious few this day, but you are one of them."

Beth had all but forgotten the Beargarden was also a theatre – the Hope. She *did* know its layout, especially the actors' side of it, like few others could.

"Before we depart, listen carefully. The King's guard are under strict instructions to admit nobody to the Beargarden unless they know the password." He took a breath. "The password is *Tamburlaine*."

Beth's exhilaration mounted even further. Strange might as well have entrusted her with the keys to the King's own private chamber. This was a challenge – and a duty – beyond anything she had ever dreamed.

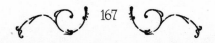

"Now, to the Beargarden," Strange declared, sweeping his cloak around him and striding down the stairs. "The King's safety, and the future of all England, is in our hands…"

Chapter Fifteen

Ambushed!

Strange's private coach was waiting outside the cathedral. Its two horses were black as silhouettes and its driver sat so muffled with scarves only his eyes could be seen.

"To the waterfront," Strange ordered, as Beth, John and Ralph quickly climbed inside.

With a jolt and a jingle of brasses, they were off. The comfortable leather seats and shade from the roof were worlds away from the open-topped carts in which Beth had travelled to Oxford and back. She knew she should try to relax and gather her strength while she could, but even with lack of sleep weighing her down, it was impossible. The thought of Vale's assassins mounting their attack on the King made her feel as though ice-cold water ran through her veins, and kept her wide awake.

"We're not going over the bridge?" she asked Strange, surprised.

"We'll hire a waterman to take us over the Thames," Strange told her. "Even with the plague abroad, London Bridge will still be full of horses and carts at this time of day."

John nodded. "We could be stuck there for an hour or more. Plenty of time for LB to make his move. The river's faster."

"Safer too," Ralph added. "Someone comes at you on the Thames, you can see 'em coming."

Beth peered out through the blind, looking at the huge houses of London's wealthy overshadowing them as they passed through Cheapside. Curtains were drawn behind the windows, and only a few servants could be seen going about their errands inside.

"Nobody home in these houses," Ralph said, peering over her shoulder. "All packed up and moved out to their country estates."

"Can you blame them?" John said. "What are they supposed to do, stay in London and wait to catch

the plague?"

"I wouldn't leave even if I did have the cash," Ralph sneered. "I'm a Londoner born and bred. We don't turn our backs on our city. When times get tough, we stick it out!"

"I'm a Londoner too," Beth reminded him pointedly. "Despite having left the city for a spell."

"Yeah, well," Ralph said, looking guilty. "That's different. You didn't have no choice, did you? You was *ordered* to go."

And I came back, Beth thought to herself. *Back to save the city that I love, and the King that I serve. I just hope we're not too late.*

The coachman took them through an alley short cut, and soon the houses surrounding them were far smaller and meaner-looking than the grand dwellings of Cheapside. Almost all of the doors had red crosses on them, and some of them stood open onto the street now. Beth swallowed hard as she realized what that meant.

"There's nobody living there any more," she murmured. "Everyone who lived in those houses is dead…"

"You must not yield to despair," Strange warned her. "Two thousand souls were lost in the last week alone. But terrible as that is, it is *nothing* compared to the loss

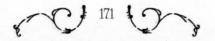 171

of life that will ensue if we fail in our task."

She nodded once, clenching her jaw and drawing in a deep breath. It hurt Beth to see London looking so ravaged, but she still could not turn away. As the horses trotted through the streets, the heartbroken sobs of widowed women and the howls of orphaned children echoed from near and far. Every church they passed had a gaping plague pit dug in the churchyard, where carts bearing bodies lined up to dump their loads.

"I'm ready," she said in a hoarse but determined voice. "Don't doubt my will to fight, sir."

The coach rattled to a halt at the bank of the Thames, close to the end of London Bridge that spanned the water like an overbuilt street. The mysterious driver didn't say a word as they all clambered out. It was high tide and the Thames lapped at the stones of the wharf. Watermen piloted their boats across the river, taking passengers to their destinations, and Strange glanced quickly around, looking for a waterman to beckon over.

But just then, Beth heard a shout from behind them, in a familiar, high-pitched voice: "This is as far as you get, you King-loving filth!"

She span round just in time to see Mott's co-conspirator, Jack Leighton, no more than twenty feet

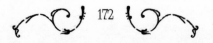

away. He was levelling a flintlock musket right at Strange.

"Look out!" she yelled, shoving the spymaster out of the way as hard as she could. Taken completely by surprise, he fell sprawling in the street.

A sharp bang rang out as Leighton fired, and Beth clearly saw the flash of fire in the musket's pan.

The shot zinged off the cobblestones behind her. Everything seemed to slow down. The acrid smell of gunpowder awoke a vivid memory in Beth, of the explosion on Bonfire Night. It was as if it were happening all over again. Leighton raised the musket like a club and charged towards them, yelling. Beth rolled out of the way, but he swung the musket ferociously at Strange, raining blows down as though something had snapped in him. It was as if Leighton *had* to kill, to redeem himself for his cowardice before. Strange defended as best he could, but the heavy wooden stock of the musket smashed him down again and again.

"Stop!" John shouted. He ran in to attack Leighton, with Ralph right behind him, yelling at the conspirator, who fell back, aiming the weapon at Strange with his eyes darting frantically between his target and the two boys rushing towards him.

"No!" Strange gasped, blood plastering his hair to his

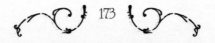

173

forehead. "Leave me! I can take care of him. Get to the Beargarden!"

Beth looked over her shoulder. A waterman had pulled his boat in at the wharf. They could still reach the King in time…

"W-we can't abandon you!" she shouted.

"You must," hissed Strange. "The King needs you! Leave this man to me."

Leighton was stalking closer, his hands shaking, looking for a window of opportunity for another attack, unsure whether to shoot or clobber once more. Onlookers were stopping and staring, not daring to interfere. But Beth saw the gleam of a dagger under Strange's cloak…

"Come on," she told Ralph and John. "He's right! We have to leave, now!"

Ralph wouldn't move. "Leighton's going to kill him."

"Strange can take care of himself. Move!"

They ran.

The waterman let them on board his little rowing boat, and pushed away from the river bank. "Where to?" he demanded.

"Bankside," Beth told him. "As fast as you can."

The man nodded and heaved at the oars.

But as they pulled away, shouts and screams began

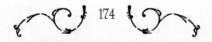

to come from the wharf behind them. "He's dead!" a woman shrieked. "He killed him! Murder!"

Beth, Ralph and John exchanged fearful glances. They were all thinking the same thing. Strange's words to them could have been his last words on this earth.

They were the King's only hope – and now they were truly on their own.

Chapter Sixteen

The Beargarden

The little boat sculled across the Thames as fast as the stout boatman could row. Beth was alarmed to see they were coming close to the dangerous passage under London Bridge, where a few months earlier they had outrun Vale's henchman Edmund Groby but nearly lost John in the process.

The immense bridge stood on pillars of masonry, with wooden shuttle-like constructions around the base to protect them from the surging Thames and from any stray ships that might smash into them. The archways between were so narrow that the water on the west side of the Bridge was higher than the east at low tide, causing foaming torrents of water to rush through. If the boat came too close, they'd be sucked in and risk being dashed to pieces against the wooden barriers…

"Can't you watch where you're going?" John demanded.

"You watch your tongue, boy," the boatman snapped. "I've been working this river thirty years, and I've not drowned a passenger yet!"

John sat flexing his wrists angrily, itching to take over the oars himself – she could tell he was still anxious at the memory too. But the boatman was as good as his word – he hauled at the oars with fresh vigour, and soon the little boat's bottom was grinding on the muddy south bank of the Thames. John went to pay him, but the boatman refused. He gave Beth a shy smile.

"Wouldn't think of taking payment from Miss Beth Johnson," he said. "I wasn't sure it was you at first, but I worked it out…"

"God bless you, sir!" Beth called as she climbed from the boat.

"Partin' is such sweet sorrow!" the boatman called back, and despite their frantic mission, Beth couldn't help grinning back.

They could clearly see the Beargarden above the rooftops of the city. It rose three times as high as most of the buildings, a great amphitheatre built in the shape of an O. The centre was the open space where plays were performed – or animals were baited. Most of the three upper floors were spectator galleries, with a separate royal box in the midst with a roof of its own.

With no time to waste, they ran the rest of the way. Beth could see that a group of coaches had pulled up outside the main entrance, but she could not tell if there was anyone inside. By the look of it, the King and his guests were already within…

She hammered on the closed double doors and they opened a crack, revealing a breastplate-wearing guard who glared out fiercely.

"No performances today!" he barked. "Be off!"

"Sir Alan Strange sent us!" Beth panted, still winded from her frantic run.

The guard made a face as if he had tasted vinegar. "Of all the ridiculous tall tales…"

"He gave us a password," Beth gasped. She leaned in as close as she could and whispered "*Tamburlaine.*"

The effect on the guard was astounding. His face shifted in an instant from scorn to deep respect. "In you

178

come, miss. And you, gentlemen."

"Which way now?" Ralph asked, once they were inside.

"Straight to the royal box," Beth answered. "We need to find out if the King is safe."

They rushed up the central stairs, only to be met at the top by two more guards who crossed their halberds in front of them. Beth whispered the password again and they were inside and, she hoped, in the King's presence…

"Welcome, madam and sirs," said the royal steward, waiting at the top of the stairs. His little beard was a wisp of silver, and despite his polite greeting, he eyed them suspiciously. Still, he knew if they'd been admitted, he wasn't to question them.

Beth ignored him anyway, looking around the royal box desperately trying to see if the King was safe. The box had clearly been decorated for the occasion of entertaining the German ambassador, and tapestries showing the royal coat of arms had been hung from the sides, while silk cushions lay on the wooden benches and bowls of sweets and fruit stood ready to be consumed.

Most of the seats were occupied by men in huge wigs, wearing clothes so lavish that Beth could only marvel at how much they must have cost. The thread in the

embroidery was spun from real gold, she was sure.

"These are the King's courtiers," she whispered to John and Ralph.

One of them overheard, looked around at her, raised an eyebrow, took a pinch of snuff and turned back to his companion.

"Who are the men on the right?" John whispered.

"Those are the generals," Beth said. "We're standing in the same place as the most important men in the whole country!"

Ralph swallowed hard. "So, er, who's that bloke down at the front, talking to the fellow with the big hat?"

She rolled her eyes. "Ralph, my dear, that 'bloke' is His Majesty King Charles II," Beth hissed drily. "His companion must be the German ambassador. Von Karstein, Strange called him."

Ralph flushed. "Of course, should have recognized him from when we met at the Tower…"

After foiling the last plot to kill the King, the three of them had been bailed out of the dungeons in the Tower of London by Strange and a mystery companion who they were shocked to realize was Charles II himself.

Right on cue, the King rose from his silk-covered chair and turned round. Beth's heart pounded with

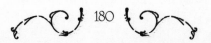

excitement as she saw the great man look straight at her.

No, she realized – not at her at all. She turned and followed his gaze. The King was looking at the bald, sweating man in the military coat who had just come up the stairs behind them.

"We are delighted to see you at last, General Courtney," the King called in a sarcastic voice. "Perhaps, now that you are here, we can proceed?"

General Courtney fell to one knee. "I humbly beg for your forgiveness, Your Majesty."

The King waved an uninterested hand. "Consider it granted. Now sit down, for the love of heaven, and remind us why we considered it worth our while to employ you."

The general pushed past them, his face red.

"Well, surely nobody's going to be able to get at the King here," John whispered. "They'd never get past all those guards on the stairs."

Beth thought of Leighton and his musket. "He's still in danger," she explained. "Look where he's sitting – right at the front of the royal box with the ambassador beside him. A good rifleman could shoot at him from anywhere in this theatre!"

"Then we'll have to make sure they never get the

chance," said John. He turned to the royal steward. "How long do we have before the entertainment is due to start?"

"Ten minutes until His Majesty formally welcomes the German ambassador and makes his address to the generals," the man replied. "The baiting will begin after that."

"Come with me, you two," Beth whispered quickly to her friends.

There was little time, but she explained the layout of the theatre to Ralph and John as best she could, rushing breathlessly from gallery to gallery. Wherever they went, she checked to see whether a marksman could get a clear shot at the King from there – and in a distressing number of places, he could.

"There are three public galleries on three levels, and one royal box," she told them as they raced through the almost empty theatre. "You can get from one gallery to the others via the stairs. I'd wager one of them will be where the assassins take their shot."

"But how will they get in? It seems impossible," John protested. "Unless they're already hiding in the building?"

Beth didn't have the answer. She stood at the railing of the lowest public gallery, and frowned as she looked down at the sandy open circle of the arena that lay before them.

"Why don't you explain more about the layout here," Ralph said, looking around them. "We should know as much as we can…"

"This is where the stage usually is," Beth explained. "It's often nothing more than a wooden platform, in fact. The galleries are for spectators who can afford to sit, and if they can't, they stand around the stage. We call that area the Pit."

"So where's the stage now?" Ralph asked.

"They will have taken it down to give more room for animal-baiting." She pointed out two barred gates at ground level, along with a large door and a smaller one. "Those gates lead into the animal enclosures. That's where the lion must be right now, and the dogs in the other one. The big door is to let the audience into the Pit when there's a play being performed."

John pointed. "What's behind the smaller door?"

"Usually, actors," Beth told him. "Not today, of course. But that's the door into the retiring room, where the actors change into their costumes. There's an entrance from the street too, so we can get in and out without having to push through our loyal admirers…"

"So there are only two ways in," John said. "The main door we came through, and the actors' entrance."

"That's right. But they're so close together, the guards should be able to cover them. Oh, one last thing!" Beth pointed up. "The stage area has its own sky."

Ralph and John looked up at the wooden canopy that overshadowed about a third of the theatre. It was painted dark blue with bright golden stars picked out on it and jutted out above even the uppermost gallery.

"We call that part 'the heavens'," Beth said. "It's for hoisting anything that needs to fly. Scenery, props, actors playing angels … I'm sure you can guess." The heavens was a permanent fixture, unlike the stage. Beth felt a little sad to think of animals dying under the jolly decorated canopy.

Ralph glanced up to the royal box, where the King was leafing through some papers and looking nervous. "He's about to give his speech. We need to take positions."

"Ralph, you take the upper gallery," Beth decided. "You'll be able to see everything from up there. John, you stay as close to the King as you can. I'll check the actors' rooms, then cross round to the main entrance."

"We need a signal, to let each other know everything is all right," John suggested. "How about if every five

minutes, we whistle. I will whistle once, then Ralph twice, then you do it three times. That way if any of us doesn't whistle, we'll know there's trouble."

"Agreed," said Beth.

Just then, they heard the King impatiently barking, "Bring me my robe, man! Hurry!"

"It's starting," Ralph said. "Let's go!" He tossed his iron bell clapper to John. "Here. I can fight with my hands and feet. You might need a weapon."

"Good luck, boys," said Beth. "Let's make Strange proud of us."

Chapter Seventeen

A Desperate Search

The only way through to the actors' rooms was to enter the arena pit, then run across the open space to the small door. There was nobody else down there, thankfully – the only thing that caught Beth's eye was a thick stake driven firmly into the earth in the arena's centre – but Beth still felt a surge of panic as she ran across the sandy ground.

The stake was to hold the lion, of course. It would be leashed there, unable to run away, while the hounds attacked it from all sides. Some people thought that made for good entertainment. Even Good Queen Bess, in her day, had loved blood sports such as bear-baiting. Beth shuddered. The barred gates to the animal enclosures looked like portcullises, and of course they had to be strong, to keep the animals from escaping. She couldn't clearly see the animals behind the gates, but from one came an occasional low growl and from the other, the baying and yelping of a pack of hounds. It was easy enough to tell what was in there. As Beth watched, a vast dark shadow loped into view behind the nearest gate, then retreated back into the darkness.

She had only seen a lion once before, when she was a little girl and she'd been taken to visit the menagerie at the Tower of London. In the cage it had seemed majestic and beautiful, its fur shining in the sun like a heraldic beast. Now, it was a thing of darkness and danger.

As she crossed the middle of the arena, she imagined that the lion's gate was beginning to rise, hoisted up by some unseen conspirator. Her mouth went dry and her heart thumped in her chest like a club. She picked up speed, terrified that the gate would begin to move. The beast would be on her in seconds, and would surely show no mercy...

She grabbed the handle of the actors' door, flung it open and threw herself inside, breathing heavily. There was nothing behind her after all.

The room was dark, the only light came from a high, cobweb-strewn window in the curved back wall. Nobody had used this retiring room for a long time, by the look of it. The Hope Theatre had all but forgotten the days when plays would be put on. It was solely the Beargarden now, it seemed; blood sports were all the people wanted to watch here.

Even so, there were still plenty of signs that actors had once used the place. Beth looked around, her eyes growing accustomed to the gloom. A row of dusty costumes hung from a rail against the far wall. Chairs leaking horsehair stuffing had been pulled into a circle, probably for a last-minute read-through. A huge chest of props stood open, with wooden crowns, tin swords and a battered wooden dragon's head gathering mildew inside. The whole room smelled of dust and neglect.

Remembering why she was there, Beth narrowed her eyes and looked more closely. Was there any sign that the conspirators were using this room to stage their attack?

She saw that the dust in the floor was marked with scuffed footprints, proving that people had certainly been there recently. There were plenty of places here for an assassin to hide. There could be one lurking among

the costumes on the rail. Someone could be hiding in the props chest – it was certainly big enough.

Check the back door, whispered her inner voice. The actors' entrance was close to the main door where the guards were stationed, but if they were distracted for any reason – or if someone caused a diversion – it would be the perfect way for assassins to slip into the theatre…

She quickly crossed to the door that led out to the street and tried the handle. Locked – but she noticed the bolts weren't drawn, and hastily drew them across.

In the inner wall, a row of narrow curtained-off windows like arrow slits offered a view of the arena space, so that actors could watch for their cues. Beth peered through and saw the King was still addressing his generals. She exhaled with relief. The longer that took, the better – it gave her more time to ensure he was safe. She still had to check the costumes, just to be certain that nobody was hiding down among the faded silk and moth-eaten velvet…

Gingerly she moved them aside, then let out a yell and leaped back. Something human-shaped fell forwards and landed in a cloud of dust on the floor.

"Beth, for goodness' sake," she told herself out loud. "It's just a dressmaker's mannequin."

She didn't really want to touch it, but as she shoved it back among the old costumes, a noise from outside made her start. A single shrill whistle.

John's signal! All was well with him, thank heavens. Now for Ralph.

Right on cue, Ralph's two whistles sounded from the uppermost gallery.

Beth went to the arrowslit windows and gave three sharp whistles of her own. All clear, she thought. So far, so good.

But wait – something was happening in the arena. A short, stocky man wearing a helmet, a steel breastplate and leather body armour came striding out. Beth recognized the crest that he wore from one of the images the Rouge Dragon Pursuivant had shown her once. He was the bearward, the officer in charge of the King's bulls, bears and fighting dogs. That must mean the blood sport was ready to begin.

As Beth waited, the palms of her hands sweating from anxiety, she saw a pigeon flutter down into the arena. It hopped about, pecking at the sand, hunting for scraps of food that had been dropped or thrown into the pit. It was coming close to the nearest barred gate. Many London pigeons were bold, but this one seemed completely oblivious. Beth couldn't stop watching, though she dreaded what was about to happen.

Suddenly, a tawny paw shot out of a gap between the gate bars and pinned the pigeon to the ground. The bird flailed and beat its wings, sending downy feathers scattering, but it was already as good as dead. The paw dragged the struggling bird into the lion's enclosure. Beth shut her eyes then, but it made no difference. She heard the frightened, feeble squawk and then a sound of munching.

Beth shivered. The bearward was heading for the gate now, whip in hand. Soon the beast would be in the arena. Just then a horrifying thought came to her – the back door was locked, and she didn't have the key. The only way out of here was past the lion. If there was someone in here with her, still hiding despite her search, then they were trapped in there together.

Chapter Eighteen

Gunshot!

Beth peered out of the slits in the windows, looking around for her companions as best she could. She could just about make out Ralph, high up in the topmost gallery, pacing back and forth and glancing nervously down into the arena.

Her heart lurched as she saw the bearward lead the majestic lion out and tether it securely to the post in the centre of the arena. It roared again, straining against the chain, fighting to get free. The bearward and his spearmen beat a hasty retreat, heading for the second barred gate, where the dogs were kept.

 192

She could see that the group in the royal box were standing up now, applauding. The German ambassador had a wide grin on his face. *Is that because he wants to watch the lion-baiting*, Beth thought, *or because he's involved in the plot?*

Her hands felt even more damp and sweaty. It was like a thunderstorm was about to break. Any second now, something had to give…

She glanced upwards, and could just about see the heavens, the wooden canopy painted with stars that served as a sky when the stage was in place. To Beth's sudden shock, she realized someone was looking down from up there.

A man, wearing black – with a musket in his hand.

It all came together in her mind like a sudden blaze of lightning. Some of the conspirators *were* in the theatre already, hiding where nobody had thought to look – on top of the heavens, high above everything else! The perfect spot to aim a shot at the King! As she watched aghast, she heard a voice ring out across the theatre.

"Your Majesty!" It was John! He must have spotted the man too, and was yelling at the top of his voice, "LOOK OUT! THERE IS A—"

The roaring lion and the baying hounds down

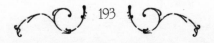

below drowned out the rest of his warning. A few of the gathered royal party looked around, confused, but the King surely had no idea he was about to die. He turned with an apologetic smile to say something to the German ambassador. Beth's heart was in her mouth, but she felt powerless to do anything.

The assassin's finger tightened on the trigger.

But then Beth saw John run out to the front of one of the lower public galleries, and fling something up towards the man – after a split second, she realized it must be the iron bell clapper Ralph had given him. It struck the man square on the head, and Beth had to clamp her hand over her mouth to stop her squeal of amazement as the man's shot went wide.

The bang of his musket echoed around the amphitheatre – even above the racket the lion and the dogs were making – and the King and his guards had definitely heard heard it. Panic struck the royal box. The occupants stood, looking around, trying to see where the shot had come from. She could hear John yelling at them to look up, but nobody seemed to hear him above the commotion.

I have to get out of here, Beth thought. *There could be more of them!*

She peered out of the windows again, hoping for an opening or that the bearward would have wrangled the lion again. But at that moment, Beth saw two figures leap from the Heavens onto the roof of the upper gallery. They swung themselves down and dropped to the floor. She saw John, cornered by the men, begin to back away as they advanced towards him. They drew long clubs from their belts, raised them above their heads – and charged.

Before she could devise a plan to get out of the actors' room, she heard a violent crash shake the rear door, rattling the bolts in their casings. She whirled around. Someone was trying to break in! She had nothing with which to defend herself, but knew she'd better find something, and fast. Whoever was out there would be through that door in seconds, by the sound of it.

As the door shook again, she leaped over to the props chest and dug around in the musty heaps. She flung masks, crowns, goblets and an unrealistic skull aside. Finally she found what she was looking for – a sword, though it was made from wood covered with metal foil.

"Better than nothing," she muttered to herself, just as the door crashed open, the bolts torn from their moorings from the sheer force of the attack.

The man standing there in the settling dust was huge. Piggy eyes glared from a broad, brutish face half hidden by a wound kerchief, as if he had been a highwayman. The club he held looked as if half a tree trunk had gone into making it. It had reduced the door to splinters and Beth had no doubt it would do the same to her bones. He looked shocked to see her there, but then his face crumpled into a scowl.

"Out of my way, girl!" he grated in a thick accent.

"You need a lesson in manners, sir," she threw back at him.

Beth had practised her stage fighting regularly, thrusting and parrying for hours with a sparring partner. She stood *en garde*, looking as fiercely confident as any swordsman in the King's army. It was mostly acting, of course, but the assassin didn't know that, and the ease with which Beth levelled her sword at him made him stop in his tracks.

He glanced past her at the door. Beth knew then, beyond any doubt, that the man was here to kill the King. And the man realized she knew his plan.

"Have it your way, then!" the assassin roared. He swung his club down at her like an angry ogre, but Beth darted out of the way and the club cracked a flagstone where she'd been standing. The man heaved the club back for another swing, this time swiping across like a man reaping corn. Beth jumped back out of his arc.

"Come here, you little—!"

The club swung at her again. Beth ducked out of the way and smacked the man's rear with the wooden sword, making him yell in pain. *That move always made them howl with laughter at Drury Lane*, she thought. The assassin wasn't at all amused, of course. He began to slam the club down again and again, anger making him clumsy, smashing into props and rails of costumes. Beth suddenly wondered if she could use that anger against him.

"You fight like a gardener hunting moles!" she mocked.

He spat some words at her that she didn't understand. They sounded like German – and they sounded obscene. He swung the club in a broad figure of eight in front of him, advancing on her as he did.

Beth was soon pressed up against the inner wall, with nowhere to retreat to. Fancy footwork couldn't save your hide if you were boxed in. There was only one place she could fall back to now.

She skirted sideways and quickly pulled the actors'

door open, backing into the wide open space of the arena.

Behind her, the lion roared hungrily…

The sand of the arena floor was soft under Beth's feet, and she glanced to the side nervously as she heard the dogs barking up a storm in their gated enclosure. The shot had gone off before the bearward could release them. Fortunately, that meant only the lion was out here … which was in fact not all that fortunate, she thought nervously.

The lion roared, rattling its chain urgently. Beth even thought she felt its hot breath blasting on the back of her neck. Her attacker loomed out of the actors' room and stood with his club ready. He let out a guttural laugh.

"Nowhere to run, little girl. It is over for you now!"

"My word," Beth taunted him. "Is that supposed to be gloating? You sound like a third-rate ham…"

"I kill you!" the man bellowed, lurching towards her.

"I *shall* kill you," Beth corrected him.

She skipped lightly forward with her wooden sword – the foil was hanging off it in strips now – and jabbed the man hard in the ribs before retreating quickly. The final insult was too much. He ran at her, roaring, and his huge boots shook the ground.

Beth waited, every muscle taut and tense. *Just a little closer…*

As the club swung at her, she dived with all her might. She fell hard on the sand and rolled over and over, scrambling back up again onto one knee.

The lion saw the club-wielding man running right for it. It leaped at him, trailing the entire length of its chain. Too late, the man realized he had been tricked. He tried to stop, but could only stagger like a drunkard.

Enormous claws raked down the man's front. He screamed and tried to pull away. One of the lion's claws was hooked in his belt. The man's struggles just made it worse, and his legs skidded out from under him. The lion mauled him like a cat playing with a rat, swatting his limp body back and forth, roaring. Beth felt sick, and squeezed her eyes shut against the sight.

A moment later, the guards from the front door came stampeding into the arena, along with the bearward. One guard helped Beth into the safety of the theatre, while the others dragged the hapless conspirator away from the lion's murderous embrace. He was moaning, his clothes ragged and wet with blood, but he was still alive.

Beth swallowed. Maybe it would have been a mercy if

he *hadn't* survived.

She suddenly realized she had to check on Ralph and John, but as she moved away, the guard grabbed her arm. "Stay here, miss! It's too dangerous up there!"

"My friends need me!" she said angrily and twisted herself out of his grasp. She ran up three flights of stairs and nearly collided with John at the top, who was running to check on Ralph too.

"Beth! You're all right!" John said with something between a gasp and a laugh. Forgetting himself for a moment, he grabbed her by the shoulders. "That lion—"

"I don't even want to think about it." Beth shuddered, gently removing herself from John's grasp and patting his hands affectionately. "Ralph. Where is he?"

"Last I saw, he was up at the top of the galleries. Th-there were more of them, Beth! He must have been completely … outnumbered…"

John's face went slack with amazement as he saw Ralph come sauntering round the bend towards him. Beth raised an eyebrow but couldn't stop the grin spreading on her face.

Ralph exhaled with relief to see them both alive and well, then returned her grin. He was flipping one of the assassins' clubs and catching it in one hand.

Behind him were five men with kerchiefs around their faces. Four of them were being held captive by the King's guards; the fifth was being dragged behind, slumped unconscious with a red mark on his forehead.

"You took your time getting here!" he joked. "This show's already over. Not like you to miss a grand finale, Beth!"

Chapter Nineteen

Heroes

"Kneel," the King commanded.

Beth, John and Ralph all fell to one knee and bowed their heads.

"In recognition of the mighty service you have all shown to us, and for your notable gallantry and valour in exposing a most felonious plot that threatened our very person, we are pleased say that we will be awarding you the King's own special medal."

The spies had assembled in a secluded part of the theatre to protect their identities. Meanwhile, the baffled generals and courtiers, as well as the German ambassador, had been told only that some of the King's elite personnel had prevented a dreadful attack.

"You may stand," the King said, smiling as if it were an afterthought.

The three spies got to their feet. Beth could hardly breathe for excitement.

"This new litter of bloodhounds will do very well, wouldn't you agree, Strange?" the King said. "Once again, they have foiled a nefarious plot against the Crown. Certainly up to your usual standards, I'd say, if not a good deal beyond!"

Behind him, the spymaster limped into view. He had finally arrived at the Beargarden after the assassins had all been taken into custody. Every time he took a step he winced in pain, but he was alive. Beth was relieved to see it would take more than the fury of Jack Leighton to end Strange's life.

"They have clearly been paying attention to my lessons," Strange said neutrally.

Oh, well. That was about as high praise as you ever got from Strange, Beth thought wryly. She consoled herself with the thought that the King himself had just awarded her one of the highest honours in the land. Wanting some kind of recognition from Strange on top

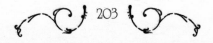

of that would have been looking the proverbial gift horse in the mouth.

Strange cleared his throat. "But yes, Your Majesty. They have excelled my expectations in every degree. I counted on them to do their duty, but I admit, I did not expect them to go so far beyond it. They are loyal patriots and more. I would go so far as to say they are heroes."

Heroes, Beth thought. She felt her heart would burst with pride. There was something she had to say and if she didn't do it now, she never would.

"Your Majesty?"

"Yes?" said the King, surprised to be addressed directly.

"Please let the lion live," she said quickly. "He's not done anything wrong, and it would be horrible to set the dogs on him now, and surely the German ambassador has had quite enough entertainment for one day…"

"Hmm," said the King.

"And he *did* save my life!" Beth said, politely but firmly.

"Indeed," said the King, his eyes twinkling with amusement. "Very well, Miss Johnson. Our valorous lion shall be returned to the menagerie at the Tower, to live out his days in peace. Being viciously attacked from

all sides is not a noble end to one's life." He leaned in close and whispered to Beth: "And after today, I fancy I understand rather better how it feels!"

Much later, they were all sitting around the table in the safe house. Strange's gold had paid for a delicious hot meal. As debriefings went, it was about the heartiest Beth and the boys had known.

Their spymaster was back to his usual businesslike self and only picked at his food, though. Beth wondered where he got his energy. There must be uncanny fires deep within the man's soul that kept him going, fuelling his devotion to King and country, she thought proudly.

"This has been a successful operation in almost all respects," he summed up. "We have identified the conspirators as a German cell, the League of the Black Rose. Most of the assassins were German or had connections with the country, like Sebastian Peters."

"Germans? You asked us if we knew Sebastian Peters' nationality," Beth remembered.

"I suspected a German influence as soon as I heard his name," Strange explained. "Sebastian Peters is an

English name, but has an equivalent in German. Of their English agents, Robert Mott is safely in custody, along with Jack Leighton."

"I thought you'd knifed that cur," Ralph said indelicately.

"I did," Strange said. "But I struck only to hobble him, not to kill. A quick death at my hands would have been too much like mercy."

Beth was still pondering Strange's mention of German names, and that "Sebastian Peters" had a German equivalent…

"Only one aspect of this case eludes me," Strange said, snapping Beth back to attention. "The fourth conspirator remains at large, this LB. While he is still out there, the danger still remains. The beast is not slain until the last head is severed."

"What do we know about him?" John asked.

"None of the other conspirators had the money to plan anything as ambitious as this," Strange mused. "So LB must be wealthy. High-born too, to have the connections he did. Nobody else would be privy to such knowledge. I wondered if LB might be code for Vale himself, but whoever it is, he has been in London recently – we know that from the tavern. And yet, as far

as we know, Vale is still working from overseas..." He
paused. "Beth, are you all right?"

A single thought was burning in Beth's mind like a
flaming torch, going back to a passing comment John
had made: *Strange always tells us not to make assumptions.
What if we've assumed something about LB that isn't true?*

"Sir, I have just had an odd thought," she said.
"Though you may think me mad..."

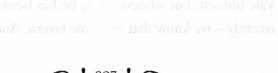

Chapter Twenty

A Revelation

It was all but impossible to sleep on Strange's coach. At the speed they were going, every pebble seemed like a boulder and every rut a trench, jolting and bumping until Beth felt her head would be shaken off her shoulders.

"We'll stop only when we must, to change the horses," Strange warned them. "This will not be comfortable. But it will be swift."

Beth wondered if any coach had ever rushed from London to Oxford as quickly as theirs. John, sitting opposite her, looked green from the constant pummels and bumps. Ralph, however, was slumped across the

leather cushions, snoring loudly.

"How does he do it?" Beth wondered to John.

"He told me he learned the knack at sea," John said. "On a ship, you snatch what sleep you can when you can get it."

Beth wished she had Ralph's gift. She couldn't even remember when she had slept last. But there was one more conspirator to catch, and everything depended upon getting to Oxford in time. If Vale's agents had reached their co-conspirator first, then LB would slip away and be forever out of their grasp. *I won't let that happen*, Beth thought. *Not for anything.* Sleep would have to wait.

Strange showed no sign of fatigue, of course. He passed the time on the journey by reading through a sheaf of reports, despite the bumpy course. Beth could not tell whether they contained good news or bad, since the spymaster's face never changed expression.

Except once. When he cracked the seal on one small folded paper and opened it, his eyes widened. "I knew it," he muttered. "It is him. It could be no other."

"Sir?" Beth prompted him.

"Henry Vale," Strange said. "This billet-doux has come all the way from Aachen. We have a sighting that

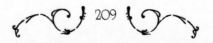

209

matches Vale's description."

"Aachen? So he *is* in Germany like you suspected!"

"I am not certain, Beth. But I am as close to certain as I can be. The man my informant saw is one and the same as the man who was supposedly executed for treason at the Tower. He is cunning and sly – but we are one step ahead of him this time, Beth."

Strange looked out of the window then, clearly wishing the coach could travel even faster. Beside him, John made a hiccupping sound and leaned back with a groan.

"Are we at Oxford yet?"

It was many hours before the coach came to a halt in the Christ Church courtyard. A familiar figure was standing listlessly outside, frowning at the strange black vehicle.

"Maisie!" Beth exclaimed delightedly. She burst out of the coach and ran to give her friend a hug.

"Oh Miss Beth, Miss Beth, thank heavens you're back! And you're well? Oh thank goodness, we've all been so worried that you may catch that dreadful ailment. Oh, but she's terrible, Miss Beth. A gorgon, is what Jake calls

her! And a harpy! She made me wait out here, said her opening night wasn't for the likes of me to witness—"

"Slow down!" Beth laughed. "Who made you wait outside?"

"Her!" Maisie said, then with a scowl "Lady Lucy, who'd you think? She's a hell-cat, Miss Beth, and you know I don't like to speak ill of people, but she's been nothing but bad. That dreadful Lord Wilmot of Rochester too, he's a wrong 'un. Hangs around the King's Company all day long, smirking like the Devil himself! There's a tale I heard from Mistress Jessop, she's the cook here, and she told me the maid Tilly saw him under the stairs with—"

"Maisie, dear, the gossip will have to wait," Beth said quickly. "Is tonight's performance still going on?"

"Should be just about finished by now," Maisie said. "She's murderin' your part, miss. Even Mister Lovett says so! 'Beth Johnson may be a bumbling girl,' he said, 'but at least she can enunciate! This wretched Lucy speaks like her mouth was full of toads!' He said that, Miss Beth, I heard him!"

"Quickly!" Strange commanded. Beth followed close behind, along with John and Ralph, as Strange flung open the door to the room the actors were using. Maisie

211

tailed eagerly behind them, happy to be disobeying the hated girl who'd told her to stay outside.

The Great Hall was lit by a thousand glimmering candles. Long tables lay down the centre of the room, where nobles and scholars sat watching. Beth recognized Rochester, along with several other important-looking figures. They wore expressions of polite tolerance, as if there was a nasty smell in the air that nobody wanted to admit was there. Beth knew all too well what they were tolerating – Lady Lucy's atrocious performance.

On the stage, *Love's Green Garlands* was drawing to a close. There was Lucy, wearing Beth's shepherdess costume and absolutely caked in make-up.

She spread her arms, addressing the audience in the final speech. Beth knew the words by heart. She mouthed them along with Lucy, who stumbled her way through the speech like a drunkard tottering through a back alley:

Good gentles all, we players fondly hope
That we have taught as well as entertained;
For there are lessons lurking in our jape.
The wise who sit amongst you will have gained
From all our warnings; but I do attest
There is no help for any of the rest!

She bowed.

Rochester began the applause, a slow awkward clap. The other members of the audience joined in, rather reluctantly.

Lucy ate it up, giggling like the schoolgirl she was. She stepped down from the stage with a broad grin and headed into the back room to meet what she no doubt expected would be a company of envious actors awaiting the "curtain call".

But Strange was waiting behind the door. He fell on her like a hawk, his cloak spreading behind him like dark wings, and his pale hand seized her wrist.

"Luzi Bayer, I arrest you for the crime of treason!"

Lucy gave a terrible wordless cry and fell to her knees. "What ever do you mean? Unhand me!" But as she stared up at Strange's stony face, she rapidly relented. "No!" she howled. "P-please, my lord, mercy! I did not know what I was doing, I was forced, please…"

Any doubt Beth had had of Lucy's guilt vanished in an instant. She thought back to her odd comments about the King when they'd first met, and Lucy's suggestion that being in the King's Company "could have its uses…"

"Hold your tongue," Strange bid the girl, in a voice that silenced her instantly.

213

Ralph and John looked at one another. "Did he say Lucy Bayer?" John asked, puzzled. "I thought Beth said her name was Lady Lucy Joseph."

"'Bayer' is her common name," Strange explained. "It's German for 'of Bavaria', the place from which her family rule. But as a traitor she should not be afforded the privilege of a royal title. Vale must have recruited her in secret when she was growing up in the German court. I expect she listened in when the ambassador's visit was being planned and passed the information to Vale. He would have rewarded her handsomely for betraying the King, and I'd imagine he promised her more, what with her coming over to Britain. She could have remained useful as their eyes and ears inside the court."

"Well, I bet they hadn't banked on her being confined to Oxford because of the plague. At least that's one good thing that has come from that terrible disease." Beth turned to the young girl, disgusted. "Your own cousin," she said, shaking her head. "Betrayed for what – for the price of a mere pretty *mirror* to admire yourself in? How could you, Lucy?"

"It … it made me look so beautiful," Lucy sobbed. "And Mister Vale said that when I grow up I could be much more powerful without the King around…"

Her face, disfigured by her tears, looked like a waxen doll melting. Lucy now looked every inch the young, impressionable girl she was.

Still, Beth felt little mercy for the girl. But she *did* feel satisfaction that they had uncovered the plot once and for all.

Epilogue

Some called him Herr Messer, which was the name he gave his landlord. Most people just called him "that Englishman" or "the quiet one". Nobody in the coffee house in Aachen knew his true name.

His favourite seat was in the basement. The coffee house had opened up the underground drinking rooms to fit in more customers, but it had been an unpopular choice – what was the point of going to a coffee house if you could not be seen?

Now it was long after dark. The German city embraced the night and all the shadowy business that took place there. It all suited this particular Englishman very much. He sat alone beneath the city streets, watching the feet of passing citizens above through the basement window, sipping his drink by the light of an oil lamp. It was magnificent stuff, this new "coffee" beverage. It set his mind racing like nothing else on earth.

If Strange could have seen him sitting there, it would have struck him how curiously alike their situations were. One master spy roosted high above the city, the other lurked below its stones. And both of them had recently employed young women to serve as spies. Young actresses, even.

On the table beside the Englishman lay a letter. It had arrived that very morning. He had already guessed at its contents, but had refrained from reading it – not out of sentimentality, but because he did not wish to be made angry until the appropriate time. His anger was a terrible, destructive power not to be invoked lightly.

One by one, people began to filter down the stairs into the basement room. They wore cloaks and hoods, which they removed in his presence. A baroness, a minister, three priests, a gardener, a handful of labourers. They belonged to all classes.

Patiently, fearfully, they awaited the word of their master.

Once they were all present, Sir Henry Vale unsealed

the letter and read it.

He was silent for a long time. Then he held the letter to the lamp's flame and watched it burn.

"Luzi Bayer is as good as dead," he told his people.

They all watched him, stunned by the news, terrified of what his next move might be.

"Imprisoned indefinitely," he went on. "For high treason. A necessary sacrifice for our cause. She had not proved of much use as our eyes and ears inside the court in any case – but no matter. Before this night is over, some of you will face death too. This is the price you pay for failing me." He sipped his coffee and smacked his lips. "As for the survivors? We have work to do…"

～ Cast of Characters ～

BETH JOHNSON

Actress extraordinaire at the King's Theatre and – unbeknownst to her admiring audience – a much-valued spy. Tall and beautiful with chestnut brown hair and green eyes, Beth has risen from lowly depths as a foundling abandoned on the steps of Bow Church to become a celebrated thespian and talented espionage agent.

SIR ALAN STRANGE

Tall, dark and mysterious, spymaster Alan Strange seeks out candidates from all walks of life, spotting the potential for high-quality agents in the most unlikely of places. Ruthless but fair, Strange is an inspiration for his recruits, and trains them well.

RALPH CHANDLER

Former street urchin Ralph has lead a rough-and-tumble existence, but his nefarious beginnings have their uses when employed in his role as one of Sir Alan Strange's spies, working in the service of the King.

JOHN TURNER

Junior clerk at the Navy Board, handsome John imagines himself in more daring, adventurous circumstances – and he soon has the opportunity when he meets Beth Johnson and becomes part of her gang of spies.

SIR HENRY VALE

Criminal mastermind and anti-King conspirator, Sir Henry Vale was supposedly executed by beheading in 1662 for his attempt to take the King's life – but all may not be as it seems…

EDMUND GROBY

Squat, swarthy and with one ominous finger missing from his left hand, Groby is a relentless villain and loyal henchman. He hates the monarchy and all it represents, and will stop at nothing to prevent our gang from derailing the King-killer's plans.

MAISIE WHITE

A young orange-seller at the theatre where Beth works, Maisie has been quickly taken under the older girls' wing – but she knows nothing of her friend's double life as a spy…

Dear Reader,

I hope you have enjoyed this book. While Beth Johnson and her friends are fictitious characters, the world that they inhabit is based on history.

From early 1665 to early 1666, a highly infectious and deadly disease known as the plague swept through England. It affected the crowded, dirty capital city of London worst of all, and is thought to have killed around 100,000 people. This was about 15 per cent of the population of London at that time.

During the time of the plague, newspapers kept track of the growing number of deaths in 'bills of mortality'. The reproduction of one of these bills (overleaf) shows how many people had died during the year, and what had caused their death. You can see that the plague claimed far more lives than any other illness.

At the time, doctors did not know the real cause of the plague, or how to prevent it. They thought that burning strong smelling herbs might clean the 'bad air'. There were also suspicions that cats and dogs spread the disease. Today, we know that the plague was caused by disease-carrying fleas that lived on rats.

During the worst months of the plague, King Charles II left London. First he went to Hampton Court, and then to Oxford. Most other people wealthy enough to move out of London also did so. The poorer people had to stay in the city and risk their lives as the plague raged on. It would have been a terrible and frightening time to be a Londoner.

Jo Macauley

A General Bill for this Present Year,

ending the 19 of December 1665, according to the Report
made to the KINGS most Excellent Majesty.
By the Company of Parish Clerks of London, etc.

The Diseases and Casualties this year.

Abortive and Stillborne	617
Aged	1545
Ague and Feaver	5257
Appoplex and Suddenly	116
Bedrid	10
Bleeding	16
Burnt and Scalded	8
Cold and Cough	68
Collick and Winde	134
Consumption and Tissick	4808
Drowned	50
Executed	21
Flox and Small Pox	655
Frighted	23
Gout and Sciatica	27
Grief	46
Jaundies	110
Leprosie	2
Lethargy	14

Meagrom and Hedach	12
Measles	7
Murthered and Shot	9
Overlaid and Starved	45
Palsie	30
Plague	68596
Plurisie	15
Rickets	557
Rising of the Lights	397
Rupture	34
Scurvy	105
Shingles and Swine pox	2
Sores, Ulcers, broken and bruised Limbs	82
Spleen	14
Spotted Feaver and Purples	1929
Stopping of the Stomack	332
Teeth and Worms	2614
Vomiting	51

Christened ⎰ Males — 5114
        Females — 4853
        In all — 9967

Buried ⎰ Males — 48569
    Females — 48737
    In all — 97306

Of the Plague — 68596

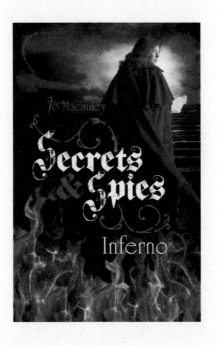

Read on for a sneak peek of the next
𝔖ecrets & 𝔖pies adventure, Inferno…

Inferno

Oranges and lemons, say the bells of Saint Clement's.
   You owe me five farthings, say the bells of Saint Martin's.
   When will you pay me, say the bells of Old Bailey...

"Sing it with me, Lucinda – it's the bit about when I grow rich next!"

The little girl sat on the doorstep of her small, ramshackle house in Bloodbone Alley, Shadwell, merrily singing her favourite song and bouncing her rag doll by its arms. It was late summer and the sun was hanging in a clear blue sky above the roof of the inn across the road. The brown Thames rolled by at the end of the alley, and the girl could see a small merchant ship and a couple of coal barges at anchor at the landing stage. A small group of children who lived in this East London alley were playing a boisterous ball game close by, but the girl with the doll couldn't join in the fun. Her thin, almost useless legs were spread out on the dusty ground before her, and a pair of walking sticks leaned against the wall. But she didn't mind. She had been like this since before she could remember, and it was the only way of life she had known. She enjoyed just being around the other children and losing herself in her own colourful little world.

But before she could launch into the next verse of her song, there was a cry of "*Catch*!" and the tallest of the boys in the little gang playing nearby sent a gentle toss her way. The girl smiled. They knew she couldn't join properly, but they always tried to include her in whatever way they could. She managed to catch the ball and threw it back to the boy, who gave her a cheery wave then went back to the game with the other children.

"That was a good throw, wasn't it Lucinda? Straight into his hands from all this way away. If only our legs worked properly, we would show them how good we'd be at their games!"

She assumed that no one but Lucinda, with her yellow hair, permanent cheery smile and cheeks painted rosy-red, had heard her.

But she was wrong.

With the sun behind the inn across the road, its doorway was cast deep in shadow – and hidden within that darkness was a short but stocky man, watching the children at play.

The inn was called The Pelican, but the locals knew it as the Devil's Tavern after the smugglers and other unsavoury characters that frequented it at night.

Soon, a younger boy with red hair threw the ball towards the seated girl once more, but in his excitement his throw was too hard, too wide. It hit the wall beside her and bounced across the alley. Just as the boy was about to retrieve it, the figure in the doorway of the Pelican emerged, picked it up, and tossed it back.

"Uh … thanks," the red-haired boy said in an uncertain tone. There was something about the man that unnerved him – not least the missing finger on the hand that had tossed the ball.

The man didn't say a word in reply, and returned to the shadows.

As evening drew in, a couple of the children were

called in by their mothers. Their ball game was winding down, and the remaining three children stood in a circle, chatting and half-heartedly throwing the ball between each other – but it was suppertime now, and soon they waved to the girl and said their goodbyes. The red-haired boy was one of them. He cast a wary glance in the direction of The Pelican's doorway.

"How will you get indoors? Do you need a hand?" he called to the crippled girl.

"Oh, I'll be all right," she said, jabbing her thumb towards her sticks. "Anyway, I'm waiting for my brother to come home from work. He always gives me a big hug and carries me indoors!"

"Well, don't stay out too late, or the bogeyman will get you!" laughed a girl as they departed.

The red-haired boy frowned and looked towards the door once more. "Don't say things like that," he chided.

"Oh, we don't believe in the bogeyman, do we Lucinda?" the seated girl said to her doll.

But as soon as the coast was clear, the bogeyman, or at least the closest thing to one she would ever encounter, was already creeping from his hiding place. The girl had her back to him. His stealthy footsteps brought him closer by the second. She heard a movement behind her at the last moment, but it was already too late. She was scooped up from the ground in a pair of brawny arms and carried quickly towards a coach that was waiting round the corner. As her captor hurried along the street, he placed a great paw of a hand over her mouth to prevent her screams being heard by the inhabitants of Shadwell. But although the girl's withered legs dangling helplessly, she wriggled her body and thrashed with her arms for all she was worth. A man emerged from the coach to help the kidnapper get her inside, and in the struggle a handkerchief fell from his pocket. Once their victim was safely inside, the two men joined her. The driver cracked his whip, and the wheels of the carriage clattered as the coach disappeared in a cloud of dust.

Read Inferno and continue
the adventure!

Look out for more
Secrets & Spies adventures…

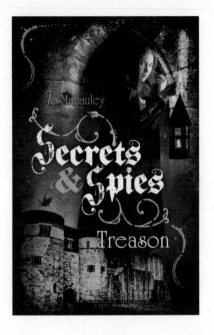

Treason

The year is 1664, and somebody wants the King dead.
One November morning, a mysterious ghost ship drifts
up the Thames. Sent to investigate, fourteen-year-old
Beth quickly finds herself embroiled in a dangerous
adventure that takes her right into the Tower of
London. Will Beth be able to unravel the plot to kill
the King before it's too late?

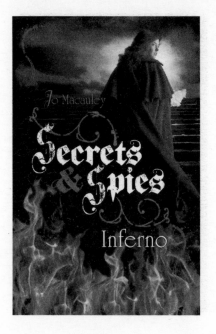

Inferno

The year is 1666 and Beth is throwing herself into a
new dramatic role a the theatre when the kidnapping of
fellow spy John's sister pulls her back into fighting the
conspiracy against the King. Henry Vale's thugs aim to
blackmail John into exposing the King, and Beth and
her friends face a race against time to rescue the young
girl – and escape the raging fire that threatens to
consume the whole city…

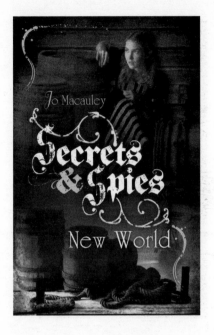

New World

When it seems Henry Vale is planning to extend his conspiracy to kill the King to an elaborate plot in the Americas, Beth is offered the role of a lifetime. Strange, her spymaster, requests that Beth and her fellow spies travel to the new world to maintain their close surveillance of the would-be king-killer. But will their passage across the ocean be interrupted before it even begins?

For more exciting books from brilliant
authors, follow the fox!
www.curious-fox.com